HONG KONG HEAT

RAVEN MCALLAN

Hong Kong Heat
ISBN # 978-1-78430-500-0
©Copyright Raven McAllan 2015
Cover Art by Posh Gosh ©Copyright February 2015
Interior text design by Claire Siemaszkiewicz
Totally Bound Publishing

Totally Bound Publishing books by Raven McAllan:

Hong Kong Heat

Diomhair Volume One
Secrets Shared
Secrets Uncovered

Diomhair Volume Two
Secrets Remembered
Secrets Dispatched

Chapter One

And hey, Hong Kong is as great as I remember. I can't wait to get out and explore. This hotel lives up to everything it boasts about. My suite is amazing and the bed is big enough for an orgy.

Debra considered the last sentence then deleted it. It might be a bit too much for her children to read.

Everyone is so helpful and friendly. And wow, you should have seen the hot-bod guy in the foyer. Pity he'd disappeared once I'd checked in. (Only kidding, I don't cradle snatch, but my eyes are still 20/20.) Ah well, lots to do and see. Speak soon, love mum x

Debra checked that she'd copied the email to both of her adult children and pressed send. No doubt if Lena were there she would roll her eyes and mutter things about safe sex and growing old gracefully, then giggle and high five her mum. Kevan would worry and ask if she had a rape alarm, before issuing dire warnings about insurances and idiot old people who wandered all over the world. Such different attitudes.

Debra wasn't *old* old — merely past the mid-life crisis age. Not that her children agreed with that description. To them it was a mid-life crisis that had gone on a bit too long.

Tough.

Deb knew why she'd resolved to do her gap year at the ripe old age of forty-four. Her beloved husband Don had died five years earlier and she'd wallowed. Then floundered.

Until she'd read an article about gap year oldies and understood immediately that she needed to be one.

So here she was in Hong Kong, in an exclusive Channing Hotel and wondering just who the man she'd spotted was.

Too young for me is what he was. Ah well. Debra checked that she'd gotten everything she might need in her bag, picked up her room key and sunglasses and plotted her route in her mind.

Hong Kong.

Somewhere she hadn't been for years and one of her favorite cities in the world. It had been a conscious choice to leave it until she was on her way home. A final glorious ending to a year of wandering the world, before she headed back to Scotland. She had almost two weeks to relearn her way around and decide where on the islands was her favorite spot, and she wasn't going to waste a second.

First, she was going to check out the rooftop terrace and swimming pool. It had been one of the things that had influenced her choice of hotels. That and the reputation of Channing Hotels.

The lift was speedy and within seconds it seemed that she was smiling at the pool attendant and wandering around a well-tended garden in the sky.

Debra walked amongst shrubs and flowers and admired the views. In one direction was the park she wanted to visit. Its trees looked like toys made out of plasticine and the people walking through it like ants. In the other she could see the harbor with one of the famous green Star Ferries crossing to TST, a junk picking up litter and a cruise liner in dock. She took in a deep breath. She loved it.

Considering that Hong Kong was a skyscraper paradise, this area was remarkably empty of multistoried buildings. The hotel was the tallest around even though it merely had twenty or so floors. That meant that the gardens, pool and a well thought out walking track were not overlooked. It was peaceful and private and, at that moment, unused. Debra made a note to use it all as soon as she could.

But not now. Now the streets and park beckoned. She made her way downstairs.

The foyer was empty except for two doormen, one who held the door open, and the other who bowed.

"Taxi, ma'am?"

Debra shook her head. "No thanks. I'm off for a wander around the park."

The doorman smiled. "Enjoy your walk, ma'am. Best time of day for it, I reckon."

"I think so. Thank you." The exchange reminded her how pleasant most people were. She stood at the door and debated which way to go. It was still warm, very warm, although luckily without the humidity that would hit the city in a few weeks' time.

The streets were busy. Businessmen and women, teens in school uniforms, toddlers and their carers. Some rushed, others sauntered or stood chatting.

It was time for the commuting nightmare that occurred every weekday at that time. People of all shapes and sizes were about. Nowhere could she see one specific tall-haired man in a sharp suit and crisp white shirt. Debra was surprised at the stab of annoyance and disappointment that hit her. After all, she'd merely glimpsed the guy as she'd followed the concierge and her luggage to reception. Why would he be in this crowded street?

But that glimpse made me want more. Grief, I'm getting old if one tiny sighting makes me go weak at the knees. Snap out of it.

Pleased with her self-lecture, Debra put on her sunglasses, thankful that she'd slathered herself in sun cream before she'd left her suite, and headed for Victoria Park. The last time she'd been there you couldn't see the grass for the hundreds of au pairs, Amahs, Ayis and immigrant workers who spent their day off sitting in the park and chatting. The noise level would have won out over any pop concert. Today it was quieter, with a few children playing ball, a group of elderly ladies talking as they enjoyed the late afternoon sunshine and several people using the jogging track that circled part of the park.

She found an area of grass in the sunshine and settled down on it to read about her latest sex on legs hero and how he managed to convince his lady that he wanted her. Within minutes, Debra was engrossed. As a child she'd often been chastised for being oblivious to everything other than her book when she was reading.

Today was no exception. It wasn't until the sun moved behind the trees and she was sitting in the shade that Debra realized how much time had passed.

The occupants of the park had changed. To one side, a tai chi lesson was in process and the jogging track was much busier. Debra checked her watch and groaned. She'd been oblivious for well over an hour and undoubtedly ought to move and think about getting ready for dinner.

Getting up wasn't as easy as she'd hoped. Sitting in one position for so long had given her pins and needles and she winced at the pain.

I don't mind nice stings and tingles, well I didn't, but hey, it's been so long, who knows? But this is bloody agony. She rubbed her legs and wriggled her toes to get the circulation back to normal.

Debra collected her belongings and made her way across the grass toward the entrance to the park. To get there she had to cross the jogging track and dodge the joggers. Their numbers had increased considerably now and Debra waited to let a steady stream of people of all shapes and sizes go by. One guy, tall, fit and blond hair, caught her eye and her heart did a weird double pitter pat.

It was the guy from the hotel. No snazzy suit, but black running shorts and a black sleeveless vest that shouted serious runner to her. As he approached along the track, she couldn't help but admire—and drool at—the way he moved. His short hair had curled in the heat and the sheen of sweat over his body highlighted the muscles in his arms and the strength of his legs. She'd bet he had a washboard stomach and a cute ass.

Dammit, cease and desist drooling, woman, you'll embarrass yourself. Nevertheless, she took a step back to wait for him to pass.

There was a grunt of pain from behind her. Deb turned to see an elderly lady, with perfectly coiffed white hair and wearing an elegant linen suit, rub her ankle.

"Oh, heavens, I'm so sorry, I wasn't watching what I was doing. Have I hurt you badly?" Debra was appalled at her clumsiness. First day there and injuring the natives wasn't a good start.

The lady laughed. "Don't worry, no lasting damage and I wasn't paying attention either. I was waiting for Gorgeous George to go by." She inclined her head toward the guy who was a few yards away.

"George?"

The lady rolled her eyes. "No idea if that's his name, but he sure is gorgeous. Sexy Steve, Hot Bod Harry, take your pick. I see him most evenings and it makes my day." She waved at the man who grinned and waved back, before he slowed to almost a halt.

"Hi, gorgeous, you ready to run away with me yet?"

The lady cackled. "I'm too much of a woman for you, honey."

"Too true, my loss." He looked straight at Debra and winked. "How about it?"

Deb bit back a snigger. "Depends what 'it' you mean." She blushed. Was she actually bandying innuendo with a stranger? A much younger than her stranger. Her kids would be horrified. *Tough, it's only a ships that pass in the night thing.*

He jogged in a circle. "Up to you, honey." He waved, increased his speed and moved away.

The older lady sighed. "See what I mean? Fit as hell. I think Gorgeous George has the hots for you. The Jie Jies will be disappointed."

"The what?" Debra hadn't heard that expression before.

"Jie Jies, sisters, people who look after the family. Like Ayis, or Amahs. It's a very Hong Kong expression. My Jie Jie was a darling. Ah well, back to my Angus and a cuddle. He might not be as slim as Georgie boy, but he won't wear me out. Mind you our Mr. Mysterious does make me quiver and even wonder if I could take up jogging at my advanced age."

Debra knew just what she meant. Trust her to fancy a fitness freak. Debra was the first to admit that her idea of fitness was to abstain from eating three extra chocolate biscuits and run up the stairs rather than walk.

She sighed. Ah well, she knew what the lady meant about having her day made. There was no two ways about it, the guy was sex on legs and the sort of man to make you roll over and shout 'play your cards right and you can have me'.

With a mental shrug at her fanciful notions, she took her life into her hands to cross the road and dodge pedestrians, cars and trams, and walk back to the hotel. As if someone like that would pay more than passing attention to a middle-aged overweight lady who could give him several years. Let alone listen to her telling *him* to play his cards right.

Oh well, I can dream. But dreaming led to a damp crotch and a need for relief. Debra made her way into her suite, dragged her clothes off and indulged in a well needed self-induced orgasm that left her hot, sweaty and pleased that she was gifted with a great imagination. Her mystery man had featured heavily, as she used her hands to tease her clit and fall over the edge.

Never had a shower been so welcome. Debra let the lukewarm water stream over her, soaking her hair and body, and reveled in the tingles that still shook her.

The water stung her climax-sensitive skin as she rubbed shower gel over herself. It was worth it and in lieu of the real thing, not half bad.

Her tummy rumbled to remind her not to linger. Debra switched off the shower and toweled herself dry. It didn't take long to dress and with her laptop under her arm, she made her way to the residents' lounge for a welcome cocktail.

She couldn't help the way she scanned the room to see if a certain blond head stood out from the mix of people seated there.

It didn't. The lump of disappointment that hit her like a lead weight was way too over the top for such a few brief glimpses of someone who, for all she knew, could be a serial ax murderer.

Ah well, obviously not a guest any longer. If he had been in the first place. Grow up and get over it. And quit thinking worst case scenarios. He might have been an eccentric millionaire on his way to Bora Bora or somewhere exotic, with a harem and thirteen Chihuahuas waiting for him in that stretch limo I saw in the street.

The thought amused her all the way through her rum punch and dumpling nibbles, as she listened to an amazing duo playing and singing popular classics.

It put her in a great mood as she elected to eat in the lounge and not bother with the dining room. It was one of the bonuses of an executive suite and she might as well enjoy it. The room was small and intimate and probably less intimidating to eat in alone.

Not that it bothered Debra overmuch. As ever she had her laptop to write her diary on and catch up with her emails and her eReader with whatever she fancied reading at the ready.

It didn't stop her taking a surreptitious glance at every new occupant. None were tall, blond and drop dead gorgeous.

Debra put him out of her mind and enjoyed her chicken and rice instead. Combined with a good dry Australian white wine and rounded off by fruit, she felt nicely full but not stuffed. After declining a liqueur or coffee, Debra took herself back to her suite. It had been a long day.

It became even longer. So sure that she'd be tired and want an early night, Debra clambered into bed before ten and turned the light off by half past. To lie awake with her mind buzzing.

Half an hour later, she accepted that sleep wasn't on her agenda any time soon and got out of bed and slipped on her sundress. She'd take herself up to the garden and spend a few minutes looking at the city by night. Maybe some fresh air and a circuit of the walking path would make her sleepy.

The corridor was quiet and the lift arrived within seconds. Not much more than ten minutes since she'd thrown back the duvet, Debra opened the door to the terrace. The area was dimly lit with just enough light to show where the paths and flowerbeds were.

She took a deep breath to savor the night-scented flowers and the warm air. From the street below, a car honked its horn and engines revved. The clatter of a tram drifted up to where Debra stared over the parapet.

The water of the harbor shone in the moonlight and the lights of the boats twinkled and shared their positions with each other. High above, a plane headed toward the airport and as more often than not, the Peak was shrouded in cloud.

Debra acknowledged that there and then, she was at peace with the world. Maybe it was her earlier climax, maybe it was the thought that she would soon see her family again, but she had a perfect sense of contentment.

She turned toward the pool area and leaned on the gate to look over into the water.

The gate opened and nearly deposited her knees first on the floor. Either the lock was faulty, or someone hadn't turned the key, because it stated in the hotel information booklet that the pool was locked from dusk to dawn.

Tonight it wasn't.

Debra bit her lip and considered her options. On the one hand it should be locked and she didn't want to get anyone in trouble. On the other, it was hot and sticky, the humidity seemed to have descended with dusk and she hadn't kicked over the traces since the belly dancing and… She shut that thought off.

Sod it, I always said I wanted to swim at midnight. Actually she'd said from a beach at midnight, but beggars couldn't be choosers and it was a perfect opportunity. Debra looked down at her sundress. She wasn't subjecting it to chlorine, but her underwear maybe. Before she had time to change her mind she pulled the dress over her head, flung it on a nearby chair, kicked off her flip-flops and dove in.

Into water as soft as silk and as warm as a perfect bath.

* * * *

Abraham Van Meister, Braam to his friends, Mr. Van Meister to his business associates and 'that Bloody Van Meister' to his enemies, of whom he guessed there were more than a few, stretched his arms and yawned. At least he was able to hand the hotel over to the night manager and think about what was going to happen next. A glass of wine and a good night's sleep he hoped. Sadly not in his own bed. It wasn't worth the journey out to Sai Kung on the mainland, just to get back for six in the morning. In a few more days he'd be able to leave the new manager to fend for himself whilst Braam had a couple of welcome days away from the hotel. Once away he'd not think about the ex-manager, the ex-head receptionist and a missing several hundreds of thousands of pounds.

As a troubleshooter for the Channing chain, Braam reported directly to Mike Channing, the grandson of the founder and now CEO of the company. He liked and respected Mike who generally let him get on and do his job without interference.

Braam was no stranger to mysteries and underhanded dealings, but why a trusted manager had felt it necessary to abscond with the money and the nothing out of the ordinary head receptionist, he couldn't understand. There had been no triggers to point to the happenings until Braam had had a phone call from head office, which had interrupted an overdue holiday. It was a plea to cut the vacation short and return to Hong Kong, try to sort things out and help a new manager to settle in.

"Don't worry if you see our esteemed Head of Human Resources pop by. He's out in Asia soon and bloody worried like the rest of us about this mess," Braam had been told by Danielle, Mike's PA. "Just a heads-up, not that I think you'll need it."

So far, Alex Chin had been nowhere to be seen, but he wouldn't be at all surprised if that changed now that Braam was due to move on.

A few weeks earlier, Braam's proposed companion on his sun, sea and—hopefully—sex break had made up her mind she wanted the sort of commitment Braam didn't feel toward her. The upshot was that she had canceled her booking. Therefore he'd had no problem in returning to his home city and the troubled hotel.

Sadly, though, he'd spent more nights sleeping at the hotel than in his house on the outskirts of the fishing village of Sai Kung. Two more nights after this, he promised himself, then three nights in his own bed. Solo, but his.

"All's well, Sidney," he said to the serious Chinese man who was the duty night manager. "I'm going to walk around the roof terrace to smell the fresh air, then grab a glass of Merlot and turn in. Ring me if you need me."

"Sure thing, Mr. Van Meister, but I reckon I'll not need to. You get a good night's sleep and I'll see you in the morning."

Braam nodded and caught up his jacket to slip his finger through the neck loop and hook it over his shoulder. A few minutes to de-kink his muscles and fill his lungs with fresh, or as fresh as Hong Kong air got, and he'd head to his room and the bottle of wine he had waiting for him there. He wasn't a big drinker, but a glass of wine as he wound down was welcome.

He ignored the thoughts about a much more pleasurable way to wind down that slid into his mind. One that involved him and the woman he'd seen in the park earlier. The curvy brunette with the cheeky grin had interested him—and his cock—more than a little. She'd stood and watched him run toward her and his body had tightened at the blatant interest he saw in her expression. If he hadn't been pushed for time, he'd have tried to talk to her for longer. Braam was sure the old lady he spoke to most days had winked at him in encouragement.

He was certain his mystery lady had been checking in when he'd been in the foyer with the new manager earlier that day. However, it hadn't been possible to find out who she was without seeming like a stalker and making the receptionists wonder what was wrong.

Story of my life. The ones I'm interested in don't see me and the ones who are interested in me scare me senseless. Or want more than I've got to give. Braam got into the lift and pressed the button for the roof. Ten minutes, he promised himself. Ten mindless stress-reducing minutes and he'd turn in.

The lift slid to a halt and Braam got out and walked toward the edge of the building. He loved it up there at night, when the sounds of the city were muted and the stars vied with the city lights to illuminate the sky.

Tonight the sky was almost cloudless, except for the Peak's semi-permanent veil and it was bright enough to see his way around the garden using the few security lights that came on automatically at dusk.

As he reached the entrance into the pool area, he heard splashing and noticed that the gate was open.

He took a step toward it then hesitated. The area should be locked and secure, but by the sound of it, someone had managed to unlock the gate. If his ears didn't deceive him, that person was swimming.

Braam's first thought was anger and that someone needed a kick up the arse for negligence. His second was that whoever it was swimming couldn't sing for toffee. The off-key rendition of 'Just Keep Swimming' from *Finding Nemo* was excruciating. It stopped mid verse and there was a loud splash then silence. Braam pushed open the door to the pool area and looked at the rippled surface of the water. A few bubbles popped up from the depths but the singer-swimmer was nowhere to be seen.

He waited anxiously as the seconds passed. All he could see were those damned bubbles. *Shit, had they drowned singing that stupid song?* There was nothing for it. Braam pulled his shirt over his head and heard buttons pop and roll over the floor tiles, as he dragged it from his body and threw it over a handy bush.

Bloody hell, why me? He fumbled with his belt buckle and drew the belt through the loops that held it in place before he grasped the tag of his zip and lowered it.

"What the…? Argh." The voice was female and not as outraged as he'd have thought it should be when an intruder faced a semi-naked man.

Braam stopped pulling his trousers down over his hips and glared at the woman who had popped up from under the water and was floating as if she didn't have a care in the world.

"It should be me saying that."

"Pardon?" She did a perfect roll under the water and he caught a glimpse of bright red underwear—there was no way on earth the scraps of lace were a bikini—before she popped up again and pushed her dark hair out of her eyes.

"Saying 'what the…? Argh'," Braam said and chuckled. "And adding you're not supposed to be here at this time of night."

She stared up at him and grinned. The moon appeared from behind a cloud and his pulse jumped like a flea in a circus. It was her. His mystery lady.

"So I am, or should that be am not?" She swirled her arms, and the moonlight caught the ripples and sent tiny moonbeams dancing over the surface of the pool. "Which means unless you're the night watchman...?" Her voice trailed off mid-sentence, on a querying note.

Braam shook his head.

"Then neither should you. So why don't you join me? Or is jogging the only exercise you do?" She tilted her head to one side and swam in lazy circles around the island in the center of the pool.

Does she know there's innuendo in that statement?

"Come on, live dangerously. You know you shouldn't swim alone at night." She laughed. "So in actual fact, we'll be helping each other."

Why not? Braam pushed the sides of his trousers apart and kicked them off his legs with scant care to creases. The suit needed to go to the cleaners anyway. An over anxious sous chef had made sure of that when Braam had checked the buffet earlier.

He left his boxers on — after all there was such a thing as over-familiarity — and dove in.

The water closed over his head and he pushed to the surface. It was like swimming in a Jacuzzi without the bubbles. The warmth surrounded him as he swam toward the woman leaning against the edge of the pool with her arms stretched out to hold her in place.

"So, hello, Ms. Intruder. We meet again." He trod water and moved his arms and hands to stay in front of her and not enter into her personal space. As much as he'd have liked to crowd her, demand who she was and why she was there, he knew better.

"It seems we do. Nothing more mysterious than the ways of the world, eh?" She chuckled and splashed water with her legs. "Is this where I say fancy meeting you here? Or we must quit meeting like this, people will talk?"

There was no doubt about that, especially if the night manager turned the security cameras on. Braam angled his body then swam around the island so that if that did happen, his face wouldn't be seen. There was one spot where the cameras didn't reach, but was visible to the lifeguards when they were on duty. As he hoped, the lady swam after him, until they reached what he termed the safe area.

"Are we playing tag?" Her voice was husky and it lifted his libido and his cock by several notches. In fact, his cock was pressing against his boxers and even the water couldn't come to his aid so he didn't get harder by the minute. This woman intrigued him.

"I can think of better things to play."

Her eyes widened and the laugh she gave went straight to his dick and hinted at all things erotic.

"Such as? Ludo? Scrabble, or, I know, Hotel?" She ran her tongue around her lips in an unconscious invitation to plunder and Braam was hard pressed not to groan.

"You show me yours and I'll show you mine..." Braam paused. "Hotel, I mean, what else?"

She giggled. It wasn't the silly sound a young girl would make, but a deep, sexy noise. "How about Kiss Chase?"

In one swift movement the lady pushed off the side, kissed him hard on the lips and turned to swim away. He was too fast for her. Braam held her by the shoulders, tread water and kissed her back.

She groaned deep into his mouth and let her tongue swirl with his. Her body floated next to his and her breasts teased his chest. The thin lace that covered her was no barrier to hide how her nipples stood out. Braam slid one leg between hers and moved one hand to hold her ass and push her tight against him.

She wriggled and ground her pussy on his cock. Yet again, the few scraps of lace she wore were negligible. Even so it took immense control not to rip them away and have nothing between them. Instead he held her close, let her rub herself on him and savored the moment. Braam swam them backwards a few feet until he could rest on a ledge a foot or so underwater and sit his lady on his knees with her legs either side and her pussy open to his cock. It was teasing, tantalizing and downright enjoyable. Judging by the shivers and mewls she made as he nibbled her ear and scattered kisses over her face and mouth, she agreed. Her hands played with his nipples.

Until his cock gave notice that a few more seconds' play and they'd need to clean the pool out. He was so close to coming it hurt.

Braam pulled back and she moaned in protest.

"Honey, I'm so close to coming it's painful. We need to get out and find somewhere more suitable." He towed her to the roman steps at one end of the pool and glanced around the area. Not even a sunbed had been left out.

His lady looked dazed and her eyes were misty.

"Eh?"

"We can't come in the pool. Well, I can't. We need to… Holy hell and fuck."

She sat up, half out of the water, and rubbed her face. "That sounds rude, and hold on, we need to fuck? Who says?"

"Well, you didn't say we didn't a few minutes ago," Braam said. "But we need condoms. I don't suppose you have one with you?"

"Con… Argh, shit and fuck. No, strangely I don't. They're not something I feel I need when I go for a walk at midnight." She sounded horrified. "Even if it does include an illicit swim. You?"

He shook his head. "Sadly no. I mean where would I carry it?

She got out of the pool and looked around her. "Apart from that, I don't make a habit of screwing with strangers, even with a condom. Where's a towel? Blame it on the moon, oh, I don't know, temporary insanity or jet lag or something. Pure fucking stupidity. Look, if you try anything, I've got a black belt in karate. So, towels?"

"Locked away. Along with sunbeds, robes and all things needed to fuck." He paused. "Or dry off."

She shut her eyes and sighed. "Figures. Oh, Lord, what have I done?"

"Nothing yet, and in the future? Up to you, but let me say, I seem to have been inflicted by the same bout of insanity if that's any consolation."

"It isn't. I guess I'll have to do the walk of shame in a dress sticking to my wet body."

"Or we could make love and dry off that way?" Braam suggested. He could have bitten his tongue out. *Do I have a death wish? When will I learn to keep my mouth shut?*

"Or not. Sorry. But I don't even know your name. Isn't it at least polite to be introduced or something?"

She shivered and Braam stood up and left the pool to grab his shirt.

"Here, use this to dry off." He handed her the shirt and walked to the other side of the pool where his jacket and trousers were. "My name is Abraham," he said as he used his jacket to soak up the bulk of the moisture on him. It looked like even the dry cleaners wouldn't save it. "Braam to my friends."

There was silence from the other side of the pool.

"And you?"

His answer was to hear the faint noise of the lift descending.

Braam swore. Long, loud and in several languages of his mixed heritage as he ran around the pool area and across the garden to the lift.

His shirt lay on the tiles in front of the lift doors. Above it on the wall, the floor indicator mocked him as it said its destination. *Ground.*

Sod it. If she were a guest, she wouldn't want the ground floor, not at that time of night. Even reception wasn't there. That was on the first floor, along with the public bar. If she wasn't a guest, how the hell had she got up to the terrace? Any floor above the first could only be accessed by using a registered room key. He was damned sure he'd seen her check in, so she was playing games with him.

Braam knew when he'd been outwitted. Sadly his cock didn't and he was going to have to decide between a cold shower or a hand job. Neither appealed to him. He struggled into his suit, which chafed on his wet, sensitive skin, closed the gate then locked it with his security code. Whoever opened up in the morning would need to find him. Dammit, that meant being awake and alert before seven.

Not in the best of moods, he made his way back to his room.

And the shower.

Nevertheless he made a mental note to buy condoms.

Chapter Two

Idiotic, stupid, moronic me. Crappy, shitty, arsehole him. Debra, you're losing it. You almost shagged a total stranger in the swimming pool of a five-star hotel. Shit, and it was so high up, I could have about qualified for the mile-high club without a plane. And, oh my God, without a condom. Am I the most stupid person in the world to dish out the advice and almost ignore it?

Debra castigated herself as she tossed and turned in the super-king bed and punched her pillows much as she would have liked to have punched her mystery man. Which wasn't fair. After all, it was her own fault he'd come on so strongly. She'd practically jumped the poor guy's bones. How she'd managed to have the strength to leave, she had no idea. Especially after spotting the tiny tattoo outlined on his thigh. It looked like a Chinese symbol and she itched to trace her fingers over it. Had he spotted one very similar on her ass, or had the thin lacy knickers covered it? How could she act so out of character? She who'd spent the last year in her mental iron knickers and avoiding any scenario that could be even remotely called sexual.

It was all well and good muttering about sex-starved, middle-aged woman hormones or pheromones or something, but what about STDs and stuff?

She banged her head on the pillow. What an idiot.

Thank goodness he'd had the sense to remember condoms and she'd had enough wits about her to bolt when she could and go to the foyer to put him off her tracks. She'd walked up too many flights of stairs to count to get back to her room, half hoping he'd find her and half not. He hadn't and now as dawn lightened her room, she had to be thankful. All sorts of worst case scenarios crowded her brain and made her shudder.

I need to buy condoms, just in case. Although she was sure her run and hide actions of the night before would have put an end to anything that might have been in the future. *That's how it should be. And I ought to be grateful I got off lightly. I don't even know who he is, except Braam, Braam to his friends.* She remembered how he'd accentuated the 'a'. *He knows me as the woman who skipped out on him, nothing else.* Not an encouraging beginning to a friendship or any other sort of 'ship', so best to forget it and move on. *But, dammit, I really would like to get to know him under more auspicious circumstances.* Maybe he was a doyen of the area, a pillar of society and a sincere single man whom the hotel could vouch for?

And maybe I've had a knock on my head and am back home having a dream.

Deb gave up the fight for sleep and switched on the kettle. It was hours too early for breakfast and she wasn't sure she'd eat anyway. A cuppa and a trawl of the English speaking television channels would do nicely.

It was her tummy that decreed otherwise. A deep, long rumble made Debra glance at the clock and realize that breakfast would be served in the dining room. As her nod to that meal in her suite was an overripe banana and three wizened satsumas, she decided she'd go the whole hog downstairs and walk it off later. She'd earmarked the day for a trip to Stanley and its famous market, so there would be plenty of opportunity for exercise.

With that happy thought, she got out of bed in a much better frame of mind and headed for the shower.

* * * *

Two hours later, she left the hotel and headed for the nearest MTR station with her map in her shoulder bag along with other essentials like water and sun cream. It was yet another sunny day, with humidity at an acceptable level, and Debra had her day plotted. She walked along the busy street, dodging pedestrians out for a wander, porters pushing laden barrows and schoolchildren and students chattering and buying snacks from the many street vendors. The myriad of smells assaulted her nostrils in a good way and she vowed not to have breakfast in the hotel the next day, but to sample some of the goodies on display outside.

Suited businessmen with a briefcase in one hand and their other holding a phone to their ears walked briskly between everyone and the whole sight was one of organized chaos. How nobody got knocked over by the tooting taxies, revving scooters and loose-chained bikes, heaven only knew.

A white van reversed toward her, making a beeping noise to alert people to its movements. Debra moved backwards into a shop doorway to avoid being another Hong Kong road accident statistic. How he'd gotten the vehicle up the narrow street, she had no idea.

The shop door behind her opened and a gush of cool air conditioning floated over her warm skin. Bliss. Debra turned to see who had the sense to welcome their customers like that. It was much more prevalent in the big stores than the smaller ones on the side streets. The advert in the window made her do a double take. Okay, perhaps it was an omen. She was standing in the doorway of a chemist shop and the advert was for condoms.

'So thin, so soft, but strong and just the job'.

You what? Was that supposed to make people buy them over any other brand? It sounded like tissues or toilet paper. Stifling her sniggers, she went to enter the shop just as the door was opened farther from the inside. Debra tripped and fell into the chest of the man exiting the store. Even though the last time she'd seen him he'd been in black boxers and suntanned skin and this time he wore well-washed denims and a black T-shirt, she knew who he was immediately as the scent of citrus aftershave swept through her. She'd smelled that the night before when she'd rubbed his shirt over her skin before she'd dashed away.

Oh, shit, no. Debra felt her skin heat as she looked at Braam. His eyes widened with recognition.

"Well, hello." He drawled the words and his eyes flashed with what? Anger? "Run out of suntan cream have we? Aspirins?" He hardened his voice. "Condoms? Oh, no, I forgot, you won't need them. You run before you can introduce yourself and we all know it's rude to fuck without saying hi and who you are."

Oh, hell.

"And it's even ruder not to take no for an answer. Excuse me." Debra turned and walked out of the shop and around the corner as fast as she could. Then she turned into a tiny gift shop and hovered behind a stand of postcards.

He didn't appear on that street. Debra purchased two cards and a thimble for a friend and left the shop. Within seconds she was walking into the MTR and heading for the train to where she could catch her bus to Stanley, on the other side of the island. There were quicker ways, but like this, she got to see a bit more of the island.

Once she was on the MTR and away from the area around the hotel, Debra breathed easier. It wasn't that she didn't want to meet him openly and properly, she did. Nevertheless she would prefer it not to happen in the entrance to the shop where she'd been going to buy protection. It felt uncomfortable and more than a little strange to be proactively contemplating sex with an almost stranger. Not something she'd considered before. Oh, she was on the pill, but not for sex, for regularity. Now it seemed those little pink tablets she swallowed each morning might come in useful for something other than every fourth Sunday be prepared. She couldn't fathom out her mindset and it was unsettling to say the least.

As the MTR drew into Chai Wan, Debra made her mind up. She'd buy the prophylactics and hope she got a chance to use them. If she saw him again, she could maybe show him she was interested, in a nice, let's get to know each other first, mature and adult way. How to meet him was going to be the problem. She couldn't very well ask at reception for the fit guy she'd seen around, oh and he's called Braam and has a tiny Chinese symbol tattooed on his left thigh. *Not likely*.

Debra left the train and walked down to ground level. The bus was where she'd been told to find it and within five minutes it had left the bus stance and was shuddering its way along the bumpy road. Even out here, the route was crowded with every type of vehicle imaginable. She swore she'd seen a guy on a kid's scooter, several skateboarders and the inevitable horse and cart.

They drove through countryside with paddy fields and trees, houses and villages then past a large lake where people fished and sat on the banks. The bus juddered to a halt at one end of it and several people got off and on. The last time Debra had gone to Stanley, it had been by a completely different route and so she spent most of the journey with her nose almost touching the grimy glass. The road was dusty and she didn't blame any of the cyclists she passed for wearing the SARS masks that were so common around the city.

The countryside changed to houses and apartment blocks lining the road on one side and sparkling blue sea on the other. Cars in driveways were all top of the range and boats moored in the bays were all of the 'if I win the lottery' sort. Debra grinned to herself. If she won the lottery, a boat would be the last thing she bought. She got seasick on a boating lake, the cross channel ferry and, ignominiously, when a luxury cruise ship hadn't even left the harbor.

The bus drew up and most of the passengers stood and moved toward the exit. Debra had checked the route on her map and judged that this was the nearest halt to the market and the promenade and followed three giggling teenagers down the aisle and onto the street.

The pavement was hot under her flip-flops and she was glad to get into the shade of the market and take her time to browse the stalls. A lot of them held no interest for her. She'd had her fill of plaster cast models of the Great Wall, or temples and shrines. However, a couple of stalls caught her attention. The first had prints and photos and she fell for a tiny picture of a couple in the moonlight, simply because it reminded her of the previous night. Mentally chastising herself for being sentimental, she bought it anyway and hurried to the other stall. Here the walls were covered with simple linen and silk shifts and trousers. Understated, superbly cut and, she reckoned, flattering to someone with curves. One dress in an unusual shade of red, almost like the sun as it dropped below the horizon at the end of a hot summer day, stood out. After a quick check of the size, Debra found herself in her underwear behind a somewhat flimsy curtain trying it on.

It fitted perfectly and she parted with her cash quite happily. It wasn't often she made impulse buys—unless it was earrings—but this time it had to be. As did a leather handbag and a few silk jewelry rolls she earmarked for presents. The underwear on the next stall she ignored. Not her thing and certainly not made for anyone over a 'B' cup.

But one teddy did make her gaze longingly at it.

"You like?" The stallholder smiled. "Good price."

Debra shook her head. "Not for me, I'm afraid."

"I bet your man would like." The elderly stallholder grinned and showed her gappy teeth. "Sexy."

Debra laughed and shook her head. "No man, I'm afraid, and too much here to fit it." She brushed her hand over her boobs.

"Never too much." The stallholder copied Debra's actions.

Was she right? Debra walked on and wondered how much of a handful Braam would like?

For fuck's sake, get out of my mind. And my underwear.

By the time she emerged into the sunshine, her purse was lighter, her holdall heavier and her tummy empty.

She wandered along the promenade toward the shopping plaza. As ever, several restaurants had their menus outside and more than one took her attention. In the end she plumped for Indonesian cuisine and enjoyed a dish of Nasi Goreng with a spritzer, as she sat on one of the pavement tables and people-watched.

It was one of her favorite pastimes and Debra could have sat there all day. In the end she checked her watch and realized she needed to make a move to get back to Causeway Bay before the rush hour held the bus up too much. If she remembered correctly, she could get a more direct bus that returned through the tunnel and cut out the need for the MTR. This one stopped at the top floor of the shopping plaza so she could head there to catch it.

She paid her bill, did a double take at a blond man jogging along the prom, and was astounded at her sense of disappointment that it wasn't the blond-haired man she'd hoped for.

The escalators carried her upward and on each floor Deb idly scanned the list of shops.

Gifts, clothing, china, chemist... *Chemist? Ah.* She left the escalator and wandered toward the chemist shop and went inside.

The condoms were easy to find, but not so easy to decide what she needed. Surely there hadn't been this many different makes and types the last time she'd bought them?

That was twenty odd years ago. Then all I had to decide was ribbed or plain, flavored or not – always not – thick or thin. She stood somewhat uncertain as to what to choose, until she saw a young – almost not old enough to know what a condom was for – shop assistant approach. Debra grabbed the nearest three packets and took them to the till. It wasn't until the checkout operator put them in a paper bag, no plain brown anymore but brightly colored stripes with the shop's name emblazoned on the side, that she saw exactly what she'd purchased. One super sensitive, one ribbed and one licorice flavored. She hated licorice and why on earth would anyone want its flavor impregnated into a condom? Who would want to taste rubber or whatever condoms were made of these days, let alone flavored rubber? It was enough to give her the giggles and she got a few strange looks as she gave an occasional snigger as she stood in the queue for the bus.

Once she'd struggled onto the packed bus and got a seat, she sobered up. The last thing she wanted was to be thrown off for disorderly conduct.

This journey back took about half the time that it had taken her to get to Stanley. By five o'clock she was getting off the bus on a side street near the hotel. Debra made her mind up to dump her shopping with the concierge, make a detour to the kiosk that sold cold drinks and spend the last hour of sun in the park.

That she might see Braam in his running gear she did her best to ignore.

She deliberately approached the park from a different angle. The area where the day before teens had played basketball was covered with large metal statues on wheels and various stalls blared out loud Chinese music. Debra recognized several statues of gods and deities and watched, fascinated, as a troupe of toddlers, no more than four or five years of age, danced on a makeshift stage. It was colorful, noisy and fun. She spent so long wandering around and gaining a badge, a balloon and a handful of leaflets that the sun had almost gone down behind a nearby building. It wasn't worth sitting down, so she might as well grab a curry from the little curry house over the road from the hotel and reheat it when she was hungry. There was live music in the residents' lounge later so she would go and enjoy that before she ate.

Mind made up, Debra set off in the direction of the gate nearest to the Channing. Her phone bleeped to indicate a text and she fished it out from the bottom of her voluminous holdall. The picture of her daughter dressed as Wonder Woman holding a placard saying *'Holding the place for mum'* made her snigger and she texted back as she carried on walking with scant awareness of her surroundings.

Grinning, she put the phone in her pocket, to keep it handy in case she got a reply and took out her water bottle to flick the lid open for a drink. Then Debra did something she'd forever told her kids not to do. She looked to her right and carried on walking.

To hit a brick wall with her boobs.

The brick wall swayed a little bit, but not enough so her boobs didn't press into its warmth and her nipples harden in protest—or was it interest? The opened water bottle jerked out of her hand to shower water over her and the obstacle, which dripped the liquid it had collected back onto her. She caught the bottle on its way downward and held onto it tightly.

Hold on. A warm, slightly squishy brick wall? With... You what? Something very un-wall-like was pressed into her belly. *With a hard-on? And the wall is wet and my ice-cold water is dripping on me warm?*

With a sense of foreboding, Debra took a step back and looked up.

"Clever you, I need to cool down after a jog and a face full of water is a novel way of doing it." Braam winked. His blond hair was dark with water and droplets hung to it like jewels edging a cloth. His eyelashes were spiked and his expression could be called nothing short of devilish.

"Yes, well, it's not the only bit of you that needs cooling down, I reckon." Debra looked downwards at his cock, which had created a long ridge in his running shorts.

Braam shrugged. "Seems you have that effect on me. And we still haven't been properly introduced."

Debra bit her lip so as not to laugh. She hadn't enjoyed sexual bantering like this for ages. "No we haven't. And may I say, flattering though it is that I have a stirring effect on you, I don't think Victoria Park is the place to advertise it." So saying, she tipped the rest of the water over his shorts, handed him the bottle and walked away.

His shout of laughter followed her.

How could he better that?

Braam shook his head to shift some of the water and wished there was some left in the bottle to drink. He foresaw interesting times ahead, if he got to see her again. He hoped like hell he did.

With that thought in mind, he jogged back to the hotel.

The doorman gawped as Braam slipped through one of the side doors and didn't wait for the main one to be opened for him.

"I know, Howard, I had an encounter with a bottle of water and it won."

"So it seems." Howard's eyes widened at the sight of his boss dripping from more than honestly earned sweat.

Braam grimaced. His state would be the gossip of the staff room later. He thought he'd better come up with a plausible excuse. "There I was jogging along steadily when some idiot of a tourist walks straight across the jogging track without checking if anyone was coming. She was looking in one way, walking in another and drinking all at the same time. Obviously she couldn't multi task. I'm lucky I got off so lightly, it could have easily been a black eye or bruised ribs."

Howard guffawed as Braam hoped he would and he knew the tone of the gossip would be different. Braam had had enough erroneous gossip about him in the past and was relieved he'd managed to divert this session. One of the perils of being 'local' and allegedly a jet setting boss. Well, he might use jets and travel wherever *his* boss dictated, but that was where the similarity ended.

Braam worked hard to earn his undoubtedly generous salary and, as the CEO had said on many occasion, earned every penny of it plus his annual bonus. However, it had made him the target of plenty of malicious rumors.

He sketched a wave to Howard and headed for the service lift then to his room. To once more dry off from a soaking from his mystery lady.

As he dressed in his suit and tie once more, Braam pondered how he could surreptitiously find out who the woman was. He didn't know her name, but had to assume she was a guest. However, he couldn't very well go to reception and ask if anyone knew the name of a dark-haired curvy woman with sparking eyes and a wicked smile. The staff would think he genuinely had lost the plot.

He knotted his tie, checked his appearance in the mirror and finished the lukewarm cup of coffee he'd made when he'd entered the room half an hour earlier. It tasted gross and he washed the dregs down the sink. He'd get a decent one with his dinner. Braam intended this to be his last evening on duty for the hotel. The new manager could take over the evenings and Braam would begin to bow out and embark on sorting out the bigger problem. That of the missing money.

He'd prefer to work on the other puzzle. Who was his mystery lady? Even thinking of her stirred his cock.

Down, boy, not the time or the place. He adjusted his dick under his trousers and, satisfied he didn't look like a randy schoolboy, or an overexcited youth, he left the room.

The trio due to play in the residents' lounge were a popular act and Braam knew a fair few people would go to listen and have a drink or a snack. He checked everything was okay in the kitchen, snagged a chicken dumpling and a prawn kebab, before filling a mug inscribed 'Boss's Boss, Beware' with coffee you could stand your spoon up in and retiring to his office to check his emails.

Then he headed for the lounge and set about the rounds of chatting to the guests and making sure the hotel staff were doing everything they could to ensure a happy stay. As he bent his head to listen to a soft-voiced lady tell him how much she was enjoying her visit, a flash of a deep reddish orange caught his eye and his heart jumped.

It was her. Braam had no idea how he kept his voice level as he spoke to the guest and agreed that the trio were indeed a credit to the hotel. He managed to stay for several more minutes before he was able to draw the conversation to a close and walk across to where his lady sat with her laptop open and a glass of wine on the table next to her.

"Hi, Mystery Lady. Do I get a name yet?"

She looked up at him and the glints of silver in her hazel eyes were more pronounced than he'd observed before.

"You told me you had a name. Braam, I believe?" He was impressed she'd remembered to elongate the 'a'.

"Clever." Braam acknowledged her wit. "So may I have the privilege of knowing your name?"

"Hmm." She looked at him and a flicker of what looked like, but surely couldn't be, desire crossed her face. "My name is Deb," she said at last.

"Hello, Deb." He held his hand out. She took it and he felt a tremor run through her. *Not unaffected then. That's good.* "I'm Abraham Van Meister. Braam to my friends. I've been helping out whilst the new manager gets settled."

"That's good of you." She took a sip of wine. "Nice wine."

"It is, isn't it?" Braam agreed, not sure if he meant her support of his help or the excellence of the wine. "So are you on holiday or business, Miss? Mrs.? Ms.?"

Cutting to the chase? Debra studied him over the rim of the glass. "The end of a holiday." She sipped her wine and watched his hands clench in frustration at her lack of proffered information.

"My status? Take your pick, I don't do labels. I'm on holiday. I go back to the real world next week." What made her say that? Did she honestly think this was all too surreal to have any meaning? Deb examined her mind. She hoped not. She smiled. "I wish I could stay longer, I haven't been here for years and I love it."

He grinned and the skin at the corner of his eyes crinkled. "Such interesting people you meet, eh?" The wink he gave was wicked. "And such a lot to do, that maybe you wouldn't get to do elsewhere."

The sod. Now he's playing with me. Two can play that game, mate.

"You reckon? There was me thinking to some people it was fair play and all that. So Mr. Van Meister, tell me, what can I get here I won't get elsewhere?"

He leaned toward her so no one else would be able to hear. Though as the trio were playing and Debra had the table to herself, it was unlikely anyone would.

"Me." He stood up and walked to the next table. Deb sat, open-mouthed and trying not to laugh. He definitely had the last word there.

She looked at her open laptop and pressed a few random keys. Definitely deep-seated thoughts to the fore. She'd typed 'sex on legs'.

Oh for heaven's sake. Debra deleted it and pondered what to type for her diary entry of the day. It was hard when all she could think of was Abraham — Braam —

and how he'd flirted with her. It had been flirting, hadn't it? Surely she wasn't so out of touch she didn't recognize a come-on when it was staring her in the face? She watched him chat to the groups of guests dotted around the room and understood there was a method in his movement. He was working his way back toward her.

Stay or go?

No contest, stay and see what happens. She wrote a chatty email to a friend she'd met in Australia and a business one to update a debit card, whilst checking where Braam was. Once she lost track of him and the lump of disappointment threatened to choke her. Then he reappeared next to the trio and Debra let her breath out in a probably much too noisy sigh.

The trio picked up their instruments and a soft melody filled the air. She had to bite her lip. They were playing 'Lady in Red'.

"So, are you my lady in red?" Braam sat down beside her and closed her laptop, before he took her hand to play with her fingers.

This close his cologne teased Debra again and she fought not to lean into him and inhale. His own scent added to the heady mix that called to her inner self. It was as well they were in public. Debra acknowledged she was in trouble. Deep, sexual 'I want to know him more and well *more'* trouble.

"Lady Deb?"

She realized she hadn't answered him.

"Well I could be. Who knows?" She grinned. "If I am, what are you?"

He picked up her glass and handed it to her. "Your soon to be lover."

The wink was wicked and she gasped. It was better than moaning and shouting 'take me now'. Debra had always rolled her eyes when she read things in books where the heroine's clit clenched or her juices ran down her legs. Never again, now she knew exactly what it felt like and it made her want to jump his bones.

"I have to go and check some stuff," he said. "Will you meet me on the roof later? Say around eleven thirty? So we can talk. Please?"

His expression was serious, and Debra knew there was simply one answer she could give him.

"Of course I will."

Chapter Three

He took her wine glass, kissed her hand and replaced the glass.

"Thank you. Until later."

He stood up and moved toward the door. The silk of his suit rustled slightly and defined his muscles as he walked in an elegant, long legged stride away from Debra. Seriously the man needed locking up. 'Hot stuff' definitely described Braam Van Meister.

She made herself stay until the trio finished the song and the next one before she drained her glass and declined another. She wanted a clear head. With that thought fixed in her mind, Debra sent her emails and went back to her room. Curry was no longer on the agenda for dinner. She didn't want to taste and smell like lamb rogan josh and vegetable masala. Peppermint mouthwash and Estee Lauder 'Beautiful' maybe. *After all, I need to have beautiful attached to me somehow.* Deb had long known beautiful wasn't her. Pretty and attractive was more suited to her.

A rummage through the miniscule fridge discovered a boring, but non smelly green salad she'd forgotten about and that was on its best by date. Deb ate it and the wizened satsumas she'd bypassed earlier. The last thing she wanted was to feel faint from hunger or have her tummy rumble at an important moment.

By twenty past eleven, she was a bundle of nerves. What was she thinking about? Meeting a strange guy, at a place where no one else would be about, in the middle of the night. Her daughter would rightly say she was courting trouble. She could here Lena's voice in her head. *'You don't know him, Mum.'*

Well it was true she didn't, but if she didn't get to meet him, she'd never know him. Feeling remarkably silly, Deb took out a sheet of paper and a pencil from its holder and scribbled a note.

If I'm not here when you come to service the room, I went to the roof terrace to meet Braam Van Meister at 11.30 p.m.

She added the date. Over the top maybe, but she could destroy it when she got back.

She picked up her room card and handbag and swore.

Her phone was making FaceTime noises. That meant Lena or Kevan and if she didn't answer, there would be frantic emails and texts until she did. It didn't seem to matter what time it was, Mum needed to say she was okay. At least it hadn't rung half an hour later.

She took her phone out of her bag and sat in the bed. As she'd thought, it was Lena. With two small children and a husband in the forces, she was more likely to call at unusual hours. Kevan was somewhat more conventional.

"Hi, Lena, how are you? Everything okay?" Debra risked a quick look at her watch. Five minutes and she needed to be elsewhere. "Do you know what time it is?"

* * * *

Twenty minutes later, she ended the call with the excuse she was tired and needed a pee. She did, but she mentally crossed her legs and left the room at a half run.

Of course the lift took ages to arrive and by the time the doors opened on the roof terrace floor, it was almost five to midnight.

The place felt deserted and after a futile check around, she accepted it was.

Stupid, dammit, why didn't I make an excuse? Because it was my daughter and she is more important and she needed to talk to me. Lena had told her that Sean, her husband who was on active service, had been in a sniper attack. Even though he was fine, some of his colleagues had been injured and Lena was of course worried. Naturally she didn't want to share that worry with him, so Mum had been elected. Any other time Debra wouldn't have minded, but now? Now she felt cheated, deflated and downright fed up.

She did a circuit of the roof and ended up back at the lift door without seeing a soul. Even the moon wasn't in a friendly mood and stayed firmly behind a thick bank of clouds.

Debra jabbed the lift button. She could have eaten her curry after all. And had that extra glass of wine. She leaned on the wall and tapped her foot. Maybe it was an omen?

Oh shut up.

The lift made its 'I'm on my way' whirring noise and stopped.

The doors open and a disheveled Braam got out. He'd shed his jacket somewhere, his once pristine white shirt had a smear of what looked like blood on and there was a rip across the shoulder seam. His eye was puffy and dried blood congealed on his cheek. He looked like he'd gone half a round with a champion boxer and lost.

His head was bowed and he stepped out of the lift with weariness in every move he made.

"Braam?"

He lifted his head.

"Deb? You waited?" The look of tiredness vanished from his stance and he straightened. "Thank God."

"Yes, well. You been refereeing a stramash?"

He looked bewildered. "I don't know, have I? I've been helping the guys on the door. Some assholes thought they needed target practice and chose Howard and Andrew. I helped the idiots to realize the error of their ways. The trouble was they took a bit of persuading." He touched his right eye gingerly. "Is it black yet?"

Debra stood on tiptoe and held onto his shoulder for balance.

Braam winced and she dropped her arm and swayed. "Oh, shit, sorry. Are you sore there?"

"Honey, I'm sore everywhere. One of the bastards jumped me from behind and then ran off." He shook his head gently. "I've got to go back down and give a statement in a minute. I told them I needed to get cleaned up and ring head office, so I could come and explain. I honestly didn't think you'd still be here. So thank you."

The kiss he gave her was soft and gentle, but Debra's reaction to it wasn't. *Blast. One touch and I'm jelly.*

Deb wanted to melt into him, but mindful of his aches and bruises, she held herself back just an inch.

"Dammit, woman, kiss me back properly." Braam muttered the words against her mouth. "I need you."

He held her so close the heat of his body warmed her. Her skin tingled, goose bumps covered her body and the hairs on her arms stood on end.

Well, if he wasn't bothered about hurting himself more, why should she be? Deb sank into the kiss, mindful not to touch his puffy, bloody cheek. She welcomed his tongue into her mouth and swirled her own tongue around it. Braam groaned and held her ass so his cock pressed against her. It was hard and to Deb, in her instant arousal-befuddled state, enormous. It didn't put her off from sliding one way then the other over it, though.

When he lifted his mouth, she felt empty. That emptiness was soon changed to excitement, as Braam nipped his way down the nape of her neck and nuzzled the top of her breast over the neckline of her dress.

"Wanted to do this all the time you sat in the lounge." His breath skittered over her skin as he spoke. "Wished we were alone and I could do this as well." He nudged the neckline down an inch and his cheek touched the soft swell. "Ouch and fuck. Wish I didn't hurt." He pressed one long, sucking kiss to where the top of her boob met her chest then stood up. "Hell, Deb, as ever, one look, one touch with you and I'm almost out of control. I'm sorry."

His look was so reminiscent of every boy who'd been caught doing something they shouldn't, Deb had to force herself not to laugh. "No you're not, don't lie. You enjoyed every minute of it." She paused and ran her hand gently over his cheek, the one farthest away from his rapidly swelling eye.

"True enough."

"Good, so did I."

His eyes widened and he grinned. "Ouch, don't make me smile, laugh or cry. It hurts too much. But I'm not forgetting that. Rain check and to be repeated as soon as possible." He tucked her hair behind her ear. "Please?"

"We'll see. Perhaps, maybe."

He lifted the eyebrow of the non-injured eye.

"Yes, more than likely. Now is there anywhere around here I can clean your face up before you go and get grilled?"

"My room, I guess. Over there." He pointed to a doorway in a corner at a right angle to the lift. Debra hadn't noticed it before. It was the same color as the walls and set back from where people would walk.

"Come on then, or there will be people looking for you before we've finished." Debra heard the double entendre and waited for his comeback. He didn't make one.

"Thank you." His voice was flat and unemotional. "So much for our talk."

"Well, we can talk later, let's sort you first." Deb took his arm as they walked the few yards to the door. "Key?"

"Key? No, no key, er numbers. Hold on." He slid a tiny panel to one side and pressed the pad it hid. "Now push."

She pushed and the door opened onto a carpeted corridor. Two doors led off it, one marked 'Fire Escape'. The other had no tag.

"For whoever needs it. I've been sharing my time between here and home for what seems like forever." He pressed another keypad and opened the door.

"Welcome to my parlor and all that, except I couldn't jump you even if you let me. I've got a nasty feeling my bones will seize up if I make any unexpected moves." Under his tan, he looked gray.

"Sit down before you fall down. What is it with men and not admitting how hurt they are? Are you sure you're okay to report or whatever? Should you not go and get checked out by the doctor or something? Where's your first aid kit?" She snapped the questions out as he sank into a large button-back chair and closed his eyes.

"Door on the left, top drawer, right-hand side. Thank you. I've been checked out. One of the guests is a doctor. He agreed I had bruises and a cut on my shoulder. I was lucky — Howard called the police and the siren scared them away."

Debra didn't say anything but went into the next room, a compact bathroom, with little to mark it out as his. She found the first aid kit and went back into the main room. Braam still sat where she'd left him.

"Braam, don't go to sleep." She spoke sharply and he opened his eyes. *Oh, Lord, what if he has concussion?* She tried to remember her first aid course but all that ran through her mind was R. I. C. E.

"I won't and before you go all worried on me, I'm not concussed just knackered. Oh and annoyed that I'll have to put our..." he paused. "Chat off."

"Well it'll wait." Debra took hold of his head and gently wiped the blood from his cheek. He immediately looked one hundred percent better. "Do you have a clean shirt or something? So you won't scare the punters and it'll make you feel more with it."

"Yeah, good idea. Thanks, honey, I feel half human." He stood up and fumbled with the few buttons still left on his shirt. Debra watched his contortions for a few seconds.

"Oh for goodness sake, let me help." She slipped buttons from buttonholes and slid the sleeves off his arms. Her mouth went dry as once more she saw his chest with its fine sprinkling of blond hair that arrowed downward.

"Clean shirt?" Debra spoke briskly to hide her arousal. It was ridiculous to feel the way she did. She was mid-forties, not mid-teens.

"Wardrobe." His answer was sharp, but the look in his eyes belied his tone. "T-shirt will do. They can take it or leave it."

Debra handed him a black T-shirt—did the man wear any other color?—and helped him pull it over his head. Then she stood back and folded her arms. "What next?"

He sighed and stretched a little.

"Damn, I'd love a bath. What next? I go downstairs and wish I'd asked you to wait for me."

Debra considered for half a second. Her pussy did a shimmy and a shake and her nipples peaked against the lace of her bra.

"Well, ask me then."

Braam knew he must look as stunned as he felt. The evening that had commenced so promising had turned shitty fast and at one point he'd feared for his skull. When he'd finally gotten the go ahead to contact head office, he had thought Debra would be long gone. After all, why would she hang around?

To find her still there, even if it looked like she was about to give up and leave, had helped a lot of his aches and pains recede into the background. Feeling her respond to him had sent the next lot flying.

Now he was almost ready to climb the peak by the steps — almost. It seemed his lady was as interested in him as he was in her.

"Will you wait until I get back, please? There's curry and nibbles in the fridge if you're hungry and juice and wine. I'll try not to be too long."

Deb laughed at him. "I almost had curry, but didn't want to sour my breath. If you're hungry when you get back, we'll both have some. There's just one thing?"

Here it is. No sex, just talk. I can go with that.

"Yes?"

"I want to go and get something to read. How do I get back in?"

Braam managed to stop himself laughing in relief. "I'll write the codes down for you."

* * * *

An hour later, he stood up and looked down at the police sergeant, who was an old school friend. "Simon, enough. I'm weary and I need to sleep. If I think of anything else, I'll let you know."

Simon Yip also stood. "Okay, point taken. It's late and my wife says she's going to buy a cardboard cut-out of me so the children know what I look like. I'll ring you in the morning if I need anything else. Take care and look out for low flying arms." He chuckled at his own wit and walked away. The young policeman with him followed behind.

Braam locked the office and headed in the opposite direction. If Deb — he must discover the rest of her name — were still in his suite, she'd probably be asleep.

He opened the suite door quietly. He could hear the TV on low and guessed it would be playing to itself. *Poor woman, why on earth would she take a chance on me?*

Braam dropped his loose change into a bowl and walked around the corner into the lounge area.

Deb looked up at him from over a cup of what looked like tea and smiled. "They let you go then?"

If smiles were rated, that one would be off the scale. He grinned.

"With a little bit of smart talking and blackmail."

She looked somewhat alarmed.

"No, hey, not really. I went to school with the sergeant. I didn't have to say I'd dish the dirt on how he was pee farthest up the wall champion for three years running."

Deb burst out laughing and the liquid in her cup sloshed dangerously near the rim. "Were you the runner-up?"

Braam reached into the fridge and took out a bottle of wine. He wanted just one small glass. "Never took part," he said gravely. "I was the time keeper because I had a second hand on my watch."

He grabbed the cup from her as she sniggered so much tears spiked her lashes.

"Steady. Here." He passed Deb a tissue and held the bottle out. "Fresh cuppa, sav blanc, or shall I open some fizz?"

Debra wiped her eyes. "Not fizz. It might shoot out of the bottle and up the wall."

"There is that. Sav blanc?"

Debra nodded. "A small one, that's all. It's silly o'clock and I bet you have to work tomorrow?"

"True." Braam poured two glasses then passed one to her before sitting on the settee next to her and stretching his legs out with a sigh. "Ahh, I need this.

Bloody assholes, and thank you for waiting. It was so good to see you in here when I got back." He squeezed her hand and she returned the gesture. "Hell, I'm so achy and weary. And so glad you're here, Deb, whoever you are." He stretched his arm out. "C'mere and let me have a hug please."

Debra wriggled and leaned against him. Her perfume was delicate and sexy. It was a pity he was too shattered to do anything about the way he wanted to feel. However, her snuggled next to him was a good start.

"Hmm, that's beautiful," he said drowsily. He could stay like they were forever. "Lovely perfume."

"Fancy recognizing it. Is that a good thing or a bad thing?" Deb swiveled around to look up at him.

He had no idea what she was talking about. "Pardon?"

"Recognizing my perfume," she said. "Beautiful."

"Ah." Should he own up? "Sadly I didn't, I just knew I like it. And wishing I wasn't so bloody knackered not to have the energy to do what I want."

"Which is?" She sounded as if she genuinely wanted to know.

Braam opted to tell her and if she slapped his face and left, well better now than later. *To screw you senseless.* Maybe he'd better phrase it a little less crudely.

"To make love to you. To discover everything there is to know about you. To see if we have what we both need." He raised his uninjured shoulder a little in a sort of shrug. It was hard to put his feelings into words. He was a man for heaven's sake and they weren't supposed to bare their soul easily. "I have a gut feeling we have something that could be more than a lot of people ever get in a lifetime. Is it weird?

Yes. Do I think it sounds stupid because we hardly know each other? Yes. Am I bothered? No, not as long as you feel the same."

He waited. The fridge buzzed as its motor cut in then stopped as abruptly as it had started. It was so hard not to rush into speech and demand that she tell him her thoughts.

"I'm not sure what I feel to be honest," Debra said slowly. "I'm scared how much I want you to want me. Appalled that I almost made love without protection. Hell, I've drummed that into my kids since forever. I used to do lessons in it. Safe sex or no sex was one of my classes. I was a teacher. That apart, I know I do want to see where we go from here."

Braam refrained from doing a high five. "Shall we take it slowly? Or as slow as we can within our timescale then?"

Deb smiled. "Oh yes." She kissed his cheek and nuzzled his neck.

Braam went from tired to aroused in less time than you could say condom alert. He ignored the reminder of his bruises that his body gave him, as he lifted Deb onto his lap.

"I'm too heavy," she protested but didn't try to get off.

"You're not, you're perfect." He stroked her arms in a way he hoped reassured her.

"Hmm, which bits of me have you ignored?" Deb said. "Shall I list stuff?"

"Nothing to list. Now cease wriggling or my attempts to take it slowly will go up in flames. Or in a hard dick." He was very aware of that part of his body waking up.

"Yeah, sorry." She didn't sound it. "Well, for one thing, I'm cradle snatching. Got me a toy boy." She bit her lip. "Do you mind that I'm so much older than you?"

What? "Woman, you do talk crap at times. I'm thirty-two for goodness sake, neither a toy, nor a boy."

"I'm forty-four with more baggage than a jumbo jet."

She's worried about that?

"Twelve years is nothing. Hey, you're only just a cougar. You're as old as you feel. I feel seventy at the moment so that works out well. Now hush. Let's snuggle and cuddle for a bit." Braam did what he'd wanted to do since it had registered she'd waited for him. He stroked his hand down her cheek, across her neck and over the material that covered her breasts. "Damned if I don't want to see you naked. Hold you next to me and stroke your soft skin. Feel it next to mine and then make love with you in every which way. Go to bed with you, wake up with you and, well, see where it all goes. No empty promises."

Deb slid off his lap and held her hand out. "Do you have an alarm clock?"

"Yeah, why?"

"Then how about you set it and let's do one of those things for a while. Snuggle and cuddle. You look so damned uncomfortable on that settee. At least we can get horizontal."

"Naked?" He injected a leer into his tone. "Skin to skin and all that?"

"Don't push it, mate. Walk not run."

That was good enough. Ten minutes later he'd found a robe for each of them and they were stretched out on the over-large bed. Braam had to admit it was way more comfy.

Debra had her head on his chest and played with the whorls of hair that escaped through the opening of his robe. He stroked her head, happier and more content than he'd felt in years. He could get used to this feeling. He pulled Debra even closer and she sighed.

"Nice."

Nice? That was lukewarm for how he felt, but on reflection, Braam agreed with her. She was right. It was nice. Braam slid his hand between the sides of Debra's robe, found one hard nipple and rolled it between his fingers. The sexy cock-hardening moan she gave was all he could ask for. She tightened her hand on his chest hair and slid it lower, as she walked her fingers over his tummy. When she closed it around his dick, it was his turn to moan. His pre-cum coated her fingers and her hand slid up and down his length with teasing slowness. It was oh so sweet torture. His fingers tightened on Deb's nipple and he bent his head to nudge the cloth that covered her to one side. His bruised cheek hit her shoulder and he swore.

"Fucking hell, if I get my hands on that little bugger who did this he'll be at the police station before he can say Causeway Bay." He rubbed his cheek. Why he had no idea. It didn't help the pain, it merely made it hotter and sorer.

"Idiot. Let me." Debra pushed him down onto his back with her one free hand, without stopping her up down tighten and relax movements on his rock-hard cock.

He couldn't have stopped her if he had wanted. Her skin was flushed and sweat slicked. Her breathing was shallow and her eyes dark as the night sky.

"Let go, Braam, let yourself come."

Those soft-spoken words were enough. He shuddered as his body became a mass of sensitive nerve endings that screamed for release. As his cum shot out all over Deb's hands, he screamed along with them.

She took her time to slow her movement until Braam knew he was drained. Sated, happy and where he wanted to be. Once he recovered, he'd enjoy repaying the favor.

He felt the bed move then a soft, warm and damp cloth wiped his chest and cock.

"You don't... I can..." Why couldn't he string two words together properly? His mouth was full of cotton wool and his brain fuzzy.

"Shh, I want to." A gentle kiss was pressed onto his belly and warm breath stirred the hairs that arrowed down to his quiescent cock.

"Deb?"

"You got it." The mattress dipped and once more she snuggled in his arms.

"Give me five and I'll repay the favor." He held her close. "Let me get my breath back."

"Of course. I'm all comfy here."

Without meaning to, Braam closed his eyes and fell asleep.

* * * *

He rolled over onto a cold sheet. His befuddled brain told him something was missing.

Deb. Braam winced and groaned—he was doing far too much of that, after all it was no more than a tiny roughing up—and struggled upright. He rubbed his eyes and tried to get his brain into gear. He needed a shower, coffee and an explanation. As he swung himself out of bed, he saw the note propped up against the clock.

I'm being circumspect and nipping off before the hotel wakes up. You looked so peaceful I left you to sleep. Hope you're feeling better. See you tonight?

You bet. He wished he'd remembered to get her full name. However, a little bit of sleuthing would work in his favor there. He had the morning earmarked for work in the office so a quick scan of the guest list would be easily arranged.

In the best frame of mind he'd had for ages, Braam showered and dressed in record time. He'd grab a coffee from the kitchen and get stuck in.

His office was his and his alone. As he lived in Hong Kong, the powers that be had allocated a room for him to use if he needed it. It wasn't much bigger than a broom cupboard, but the views over the rooftops to the harbor and Kowloon made up for that.

Braam scanned his emails and made a note of a few things to follow up. It seemed that someone thought they'd sighted the missing now ex manager in the Bahamas, in one of their hotels for goodness' sake. Would he be so stupid? On reflection, Braam thought the idiot might well be. After all, to steal that amount of money from a company like Channing with all their power and influence struck him as more than stupid.

He opened a document and set about collating what he had. Soon he was immersed in the trail he'd found — which didn't go to the Bahamas.

When the phone rang he jumped and his fingers slipped over the keyboard. A sentence of *4y5cvzdjyukwe* wasn't helpful. He deleted it with one hand as he picked the handset up with the other.

Ten minutes later, he ended the call and closed the document. His work was paying off and if everything went to plan, Mr. Embezzler, ex-manager, would be brought to justice.

Something niggled the back of Braam's mind.

Deb, Deb who? He pulled up the guest list and scanned it rapidly.

One name jumped out and slugged him hard in the gut. The words wavered and reformed as his eyes clouded over and cleared.

Mrs. Debra Scotburn.

Mrs.? She hadn't mentioned anything about being married or where her husband was. Okay, she had mentioned kids, but no other half.

Braam shut down the guest list, drank the dregs of his stone cold coffee and resisted throwing the mug at the wall.

Dammit all to hell. What a mess.

* * * *

Debra stood at the bottom of the central escalator that was used by thousands of people every day to get up and down the mid-levels. The lower part of Hong Kong's famous Peak was residential and almost horizontal. The escalator—in fact six escalators and three moving walkways—was a way to get people up and down to work. As long as you went down before ten a.m. and came back up at least twenty minutes later when the direction of them was reversed every day.

When Debra had visited Hong Kong years before, she'd ridden them to the very top and come back down the series of steps, which ran beside it and created a vibrant busy thoroughfare. This time she intended to take her time going up then meander back toward the hotel via a couple of parks and a tram. If anything caught her eye, she'd step off the escalator and check it out.

A group of teenagers, chattering and making a noise like a flock of parrots, got on in front of her. Their backpacks sported every tiny cuddly toy known to man—or woman—and probably a few besides. One grotesque red and purple bunch of fur that hung from an orange bag was enough to give you nightmares or a migraine. Deb turned away.

Everywhere she looked was busy, different and fascinating. Some of the adverts on the shop windows she passed as she was taken upwards made her giggle. People sat on walls, jostled for position in fast food shop doorways and haggled at the various stalls that lined part of the street. From her position high above street level, Debra saw it all.

The spicy smells of curries and ginger vied with exhaust fumes and cigarette smoke. Adverts were in several languages and people apologized for bumping into each other in several more.

It was fantastic. She rode upwards for several minutes until a shop on one of the side streets caught her eye. Debra exited the escalator as soon as she could and walked down the steps and back to the shop.

'Wu's Teas. For every occasion and every ailment. Let us help you'.

I wonder if they have anything for indecision? And a black eye? She wandered into the tiny shop, to be greeted by a smiling lady.

Half an hour and several cups of tea later, poured out for her in an elaborate ceremony that if she had allowed would have gone on much longer, she emerged with sundry packets of tea and two tiny teapots. Each mixture was made for one specific ailment or occasion. The dark almost black pungent leaves she was told would be right and proper for cuts and bruises almost overpowered her. The sweeter one—for indecision and affairs of the heart—she thought might make her sick, but she'd bought it anyway. You never knew if something like that might come in handy, especially the way she was feeling at the moment.

The third packet the lady had pressed into her hands once Debra had completed her transaction. She leaned in closer, giving Debra the chance to experience the smell of expensive oolong.

"For your man," the woman said and winked. "So he forgets the day and enjoys the night."

Deb smiled and said thank you. Once she was away from the shop and back on the escalator, she peered into the highly decorated bag that held the teas. And choked.

In cursive script and Chinese characters, it proclaimed. *For erectile dysfunction owing to stress and overwork. Get it up with Wu's.* Even through the paper bag it was sealed in it smelled like overripe silage. Debra bit back a giggle and found a plastic bag to put it in to help lock in the smell. She didn't want people looking at her and wondering why she smelled so noxious.

Bad though it was, the aroma reminded her that she was ready for a drink and something to eat. Debra left the escalator once more and wandered along a narrow road, dodging bikes and barrows and people in a hurry.

Not far down the road, a restaurant with a row of tables outside caught her eye. To eat, drink and people-watch sounded perfect to her.

She levered herself up onto one of the high stools and studied the menu. A tall, elegant Chinese girl with long dark hair, which swung in a plait almost to her waist, came up with her order pad. She was cheerful, friendly and gregarious and according to her name badge, rejoiced in the unlikely name of 'Shade'. Within seconds of taking Debra's order, she'd elicited the information that Debra was on holiday and that she was staying at the Channing in Causeway Bay.

She'd make a great inquisitor. Debra was amused at how easily she'd imparted the information. It wasn't like her to be so open. *I seem to be doing a lot lately that's new to me.*

"Ohh, the Channing, eh? Lucky you. Have you bumped into Braam Van Meister yet? I hear he's back in town. What a physique and hot, hot, hot. Mind you, his reputation goes before him. Love 'em and leave 'em Van M we call him. A girl in every hotel."

Chapter Four

The animals in the tiny zoo jumped about and screeched at the groups of people standing outside their cages and peering in. Debra was oblivious. How she had found her way to the botanical gardens and into the area where the zoo was, she had no idea.

She'd eaten her steak and salad without tasting any of it and her glass of wine could have been vinegar.

Shade's words reverberated around her mind.

'A girl in every hotel. Mr. Love 'em and leave 'em. His reputation goes before him.'

Had Shade looked malicious, or shifty-eyed? Debra couldn't remember, but why would she lie to a perfect stranger? There was no rhyme or reason to it.

Debra felt sick. In front of her, the ring-tailed lemurs were entertaining the crowds. Tiny schoolchildren, immaculately dressed in tracksuits and baseball caps, shrieked and giggled at the animals' antics. She merely stared.

Was she purely a statistic? A notch on his bedpost or whatever? Thank goodness she hadn't told him more than her first name. Whilst he was around, she'd make sure not to be. Days out, food in her room and sadly, unless she was certain it was safe, no swimming, or Victoria Park.

It was a bummer. Deb hadn't felt as lost or down since her husband died. She knew it was silly to experience such extreme emotions about someone she hardly knew, but who could help how they felt? She certainly couldn't.

If I do bump into him, I'll tell him what for and give him it as well. As well as my knee in his nuts and a jab to his cock. She bit her lip. She could still feel the silky soft skin, with the hard aroused core under it, as it slid through her fingers and he moaned his arousal.

Bastard, I'm not a statistic, I'm a person. She couldn't even find any comfort in the knowledge that they hadn't actually made love, she'd just given him a hand job. Even though she'd wanted to make love, to feel him inside her and come as he touched her and filled her. It had taken every bit of her determination to leave him sleeping that morning. Only the look of exhaustion had stopped Debra waking him up and carrying on where they'd left off.

Now she had to take satisfaction from that.

Eventually common sense restored her humor somewhat. After all, she wasn't the first person to fall for a corny line or ten and she wouldn't be the last. Debra was also honest enough to admit to herself that she'd started it all. If she hadn't come on to him in the first place, none of this would have happened.

Lesson learned, keep your mouth and your legs shut. With that in mind, Debra intended to enjoy the rest of the day.

After consulting her map, she made her way downhill and past the Peak tram station, until she reached Hong Kong Park.

It was as busy as the botanical gardens, but had a quieter clientele. More older couples strolled between the carp ponds and amongst the flowerbeds and fountains, than school parties walking in formation along the wide pathways.

Debra stopped to take a picture of a deep red flowering bush—she couldn't understand the label and made a note to check it out on the net later. A tap on her arm made her jump. Her pulse sped up and her mouth became dry.

She turned to see a pretty teenager holding a camera.

Of course it won't be him. Get a life.

"Please, a picture with you?" The girl smiled. "My friend will take it."

Debra blinked. She knew some people liked pictures of anyone, but so far it hadn't happened to her. However, she nodded and stood next to them in turn whilst they snapped away.

The incident amused her. She must tell Lena that someone had thought her mum photogenic enough to want her to pose with them. Debra took several pictures herself—landscape, not portrait—and made her way out of the park and toward the nearest tram. A tram ride to rattle her bones and a visit to the supermarket to get food for dinner before she holed up in her room.

It was annoying to feel she had to, but Debra knew enough about herself to know she'd be best not to meet Braam before her temper cooled down. She didn't lose it often but when she did, everyone around ran for cover. Therefore the supermarket it had to be.

The trouble was, Debra thought as she wandered up and down the aisles of the enormous basement supermarket an hour or so later, she didn't know what she fancied, except damned Braam and he was off the menu. She settled for a cooked chicken and a mixed salad. Healthy and nutritious. Then she spoiled all her good intentions with a wedge of gateau smothered in cream and a large bar of chocolate. Sadly she knew the chocolate wouldn't taste the same as at home, but she'd cope.

She felt like a secret agent—or someone up to no good as she entered the hotel later. One doorman was busy hailing a taxi for a customer and the other was wheeling five suitcases and several suit carriers into one of the lifts.

Debra waited until its doors had closed and called a different one. She got to her floor without it stopping and when the doors opened looked out into the corridor with caution. It was empty apart from a cleaner's trolley at the opposite end of the corridor to her suite.

Numpty, she berated herself. *There is no earthly reason why Braam should be lurking on your floor, especially at this hour. Get a grip.* Nevertheless she still made it into her room in record time. And hated herself for scuttling as if she was in the wrong.

Frustrated both mentally and emotionally and getting more annoyed with herself by the minute, Debra poured a large glass of wine and took a long, leisurely shower. It didn't cool her temper, but it did go a long way to cooling her ardor and her skin. By the time she'd toweled off, dressed in a long, loose kaftan and dried her hair, she was in a happier frame of mind.

Debra sang along—off key—to an old James Taylor song on her iPod as she plated her dinner and sat on a high stool at the kitchen area work surface that doubled as a table. She propped her guidebook up against the pepper mill and plotted her next day's activities.

She hadn't been to Sai Kung on her last visit, owing to the distance from the center of the city. This time she had promised herself she would go there. So tomorrow was Sai Kung day via the MTR and a green minibus. Once she'd finished her simple, and to be honest boring meal, Debra worked out her route. There were a couple of options and she thought she might go one way and back the other. Pleased that she'd sorted the next day with an excursion well away from the hotel, Debra opened her laptop.

One of the good things about Wi-Fi was that she could tune in to her favorite radio station from home. Listening to golden oldies and singing away, often with the wrong words, as well as answering trivia questions was a perfect way to pass the time as she wrote her diary—without reference to Braam or Shade's revelations.

The knock on the door was unexpected and startled her. Debra looked at it as if somehow she could see through the wood and find out who was on the other side. The next knock was louder.

Had she omitted to put the 'do not disturb' light on? When the third knock sounded, Debra stood up, irritated and ready to tear a strip off someone who didn't take silence for an answer.

She forgot there was a security peephole and pulled the door open, saw who was on the other side and went to slam it.

"Fuck off."

"Naughty, naughty." Braam put his shoe-clad foot between door and jamb and held it open. He bet she wished she'd remembered to put the chain on, or at least look through the peephole. Then he reckoned he could have hammered until he put a hole in the paneling or she called security and she wouldn't have opened the door. He hadn't needed his hand over the peephole or his rough "Housekeeping" statement.

"I wonder what *Mr.* Scotburn would say if he heard that language coming out of his wife's mouth and if he would condone your behavior of the last few days. Does he get a kick out of knowing what his wife's up to?" Braam could hardly believe the vitriol spilling out of his mouth. Every nasty thought he'd had since seeing her name in the guest register bubbled up and demanded to be said.

"I wouldn't think so." Debra's hazel eyes were almost black and as he glared at her, tears appeared and clouded them.

Ha, a woman's wiles, what next?

"He'd be hard pressed to make any comment unless he can speak from the grave. And that would be difficult, he was cremated." Deb sniffed and wiped her eyes with the back of her hand. "Please take your foot out of the door. You're hardly one to talk. What was it the waitress said? Oh, yes, I remember. *'Have you bumped into Braam Van Meister yet? I hear he's back in town. My god what a man and hot, hot, hot. Mind you, his reputation goes before him. Love 'em and leave 'em Van M we call him. A girl in every hotel'.*" She glared at him. Her voice rose to a shout. "Now move your bloody foot."

"What? A what?" Braam blinked and shook his head. Where had she got that load of crap from? "I've had one partner—girlfriend, call it what you will—in three years. This bloody job is not good for cementing relationships, *Mrs.* Scotburn. And that one single one ground to a halt a while back, because she wanted commitment and I didn't. Then I met you and fell hook, line and sinker and why the fuck am I having this conversation in a hotel corridor where anyone can hear?"

"Because I don't want to invite a homicidal serial player into my room?" Debra stood back. "But you, I'll give you the benefit of doubt. Come in, you're making my doorway look untidy."

Braam chuckled. She had a way with words that deflated his anger as fast as it had risen. The news about her husband had shocked him almost as much as his over the top jumping to conclusions had disgusted him. To say he'd been hurt because he was sure she was someone who was about to be important in his life was no excuse. He had a major apology to make and eating crow was never pleasant.

"Thank you," he said sincerely. "I appreciate the chance to apologize and make amends."

Debra closed the door behind him and sat back on the settee. She didn't invite him to join her. "I hope I appreciate the apology. So?"

So, she wasn't going to make it easy and why should she? He was in the wrong.

"I didn't know your name, I looked at the guest register and saw you were registered as Mrs., and I was gutted. The first woman in ages—and I mean ages—I've felt more than a mild interest in was married. Yeah. If I had a punch bag handy, it'd be in bits. Luckily I stopped myself putting a hole in the wall with my fist. All I could think was why?"

Debra stood up and opened the fridge. "Wine?"

"Oh." Braam brought his mind back to the present and thought about what she'd said. *She's not married. Oh, hell, hope she's not in mourning. Surely not?* "Yes, please, I'm now off for one day and two nights. Bliss."

"Congratulations, now talk."

So his lady wasn't going to let him off lightly and why should she?

"May I sit down?" He kept his voice flat and unemotional. She stared at him steadily until he felt like a schoolboy called to the headmistress's office. Did she give the cane? Seven strokes? He winced. He wasn't into pain, and he well remembered the cane at school. He hadn't been the best-behaved child.

"Of course."

Oh, starched and proper. He could do the same. Braam smiled and inclined his head. "Thank you." He hitched his suit trousers over his knees and crossed one leg over the other. An action he knew would stretch the expensive material over his groin. She looked down, toward his cock very briefly, colored and looked away. His cock had responded with predictable interest the minute he was near her. He was going to have to get that reaction under control, or it was going to cause a lot of embarrassment.

"Seriously, Deb, I know I overreacted, but damn it was a punch to the gut. I've never had such an immediate positive reaction to anyone." He took a gamble. "Hell, I if ever I get within touching distance of you I get a hard-on that would break glass."

That made her giggle and take his glass from him. "It's as well the coffee table is veneer then, eh? Shall I get you a plastic tumbler for your wine?"

"No thanks." He took his glass back. "I think I can control myself enough not to succumb." He hoped. "Can we start again?"

She shook her head.

What? Braam wouldn't have believed the sense of gloom and doom that filled him. His skin crawled and tiny black dots danced across his eyes. Surely she didn't mean it was the end?

"But we can move forward. The details in the hotel register are from my passport. I haven't needed to renew it since Don died. It's seven years into a ten year passport. Don died five years ago. It's never mattered before."

Braam took a deep breath. "And it does now?"

"You tell me."

He wanted to high five and punch the air. "Not now it doesn't. Not now that I know."

How could she describe the intense relief that flowed through her? The tension that she hadn't even perceived earlier in her deflated like a popped balloon.

"How can two supposedly intelligent adults screw up so badly?" she asked. "Too much too fast?"

"I guess we didn't exactly do much talking, did we?" Braam said. "And I'm so bloody knackered I'd sound like a monkey on speed if I tried to do much talking now. How about we go out tomorrow? Have you been to Lamma?" He stood up and stretched and the hem of his shirt rose and gave Debra a much too brief glimpse of tanned bare flesh.

Debra promptly discarded her half-made plans. She'd heard of Lamma Island and the fabulous track that took you over the hills from one tiny port to another, but had regretfully accepted she didn't want to do the trek alone. And who knew? If he wore shorts and a T-shirt, she could have a good lusting session.

"I haven't but I'd love to," she said honestly.

"Then can you be ready for ten?"

"Of course."

"Good. Wear trainers and bring a swimsuit and a towel. We'll walk from east to north. Most people do it the other way, but I prefer to end up where there are more ferries back." He stood up. "I'd better go and let you get some sleep."

Debra bit her lip and took a deep breath. "I'd much prefer you to stay." She looked at his face and hoped her anxiety didn't show. The last thing she wanted to do was come across as pushy and needy. However, something told her if she didn't say what she meant and show how she felt, Braam would be a perfect—and annoying—gentleman and leave after a chaste kiss on her cheek.

Why? They were both well past the age of consent, he wanted her, she wanted him and she'd gotten several packets of condoms to try out. Maybe not the licorice ones, though.

"If I stay, you won't get much sleep," Braam said and rolled his eyes. "Shit, I must be more tired than I thought. I sound like some hackneyed, clichéd, old roué in one of those books my mum read years ago. It's true, though. I want to make love to you so much, I have aches of a different kind to the ones forced on me yesterday."

"Yesterday's I can't do much about except offer you arnica. Today's? Well, who knows? Maybe between us we can sort those out." Debra couldn't believe her temerity since she met him. When had she learned to be so direct?

When I realized Braam was being noble. I don't want noble, I want nobbled. Argh. Debra mentally shook her head. Enough already.

"Ah, Deb, I want that, boy do I want that. You know I made a visit to a certain shop today, but I don't have the purchases with me. So..." His voice trailed off and he raised one shoulder in a half shrug.

"So." She got up and opened the holdall she'd carried around all day, took out the gaudy paper bag and handed it to Braam.

"I went into a different branch."

The smile that spread over his face as he looked inside the bag was all she could have hoped for.

"Well, who am I to make you have a wasted journey?" He pulled the packets out and laughed. "Ah, thank you for your assumptions about my prowess and staying power. I'm not that good, but I'll give it my best shot."

Debra grinned and giggled. "Well, it had been so long since I bought anything like that, way back then there was only one sort. So I hedged my bets." She sniggered. *We must look like a pair of loons, grinning like idiots.*

Braam sobered. He put the package on the table and tugged Debra toward him and held her in the circle of his arms.

"Are you sure? I know I want to make love to you, bury myself inside you and feel you shatter around me. I want to explore what we could have. However, it's a big decision and once we start, I'll want to carry on and discover every little thing. Are you okay with that?"

"Yes." She'd never been more certain. "Mind you, I'll warn you now, you do *not* touch my feet. I hate that and I have been known to kick out without any thought of what's in the way."

Braam rubbed his chin over the top of her head. "I'll consider myself warned."

They stood like that for several minutes. Then he moved closer until their bodies were touching. Even through both of their clothes, Debra felt his chest move up and down with each breath he took and his cock stir as her tummy rested over it. If she was a few inches taller and it was her pussy that teased it, that would be perfect.

What about stripping and stuff? Oh, God, this is a minefield. I'm on the wrong side of forty and my wobbly bits sure do wobble. Would he mind if I went into the bathroom to get undressed? But then what do I wear? My Dr Who jammies aren't exactly seduction central and my posh undies are in the wash. Will the hotel robe do like last night? But then he fell sleep and was it…?

"I can see those cogs going round a hundred to the dozen. Whatever it is that's worrying you, please tell me. Please?" He tipped her head up by putting his hand under her chin. Debra had no option but to look him in the eyes.

"My wobbly bits," she said in a rush before she lost courage. "I'm mid-forties, had two kids, eaten a lot of chocolate and drunk far too much wine. My idea of exercise is to open another bottle. You're younger, fitter and, well, I guess I'm scared you won't like what you see."

"Aw, honey." Braam rubbed his hands over her shoulders and back. "It works both ways, you know. What if my running has made my calves too big, or my stomach is hanging over my belt? What if my cock is too big, small, thick, thin, or doesn't fill you like you want it to? The world is full of a lot of ifs. So what if we say sod the lot of them? I'll take my shirt off, you do yours." He flicked open his shirt buttons one by one.

The sight of his chest as it was slowly uncovered made Debra clench her vagina muscles. It was that or squirm as her juices gathered and reminded her she was a woman. One who so appreciated the sight of a tanned and sculpted man's chest.

"I, er." She cleared her throat. "I'm not wearing a shirt. I've got a dress on."

He leered and waved one hand in the air in a 'so what'? gesture. "That's a heads-up to me then. Off… Off… Off…" The chant made her smile.

In for a penny. She grabbed the hem of her dress and pulled it over her head before she chickened out. The cool air conditioning made her shiver.

"Now you."

Braam dipped his head. "My pleasure." He undid the button at the top of his trousers and slid the zip down as far as it would go.

Oh, no. You're wrong. It's my pleasure.

He glanced up and his eyes twinkled as he watched her circle her lips with her tongue. Debra's mouth was dry. She picked up her wine and took a hefty swig, as he pushed his trousers over his hips.

Either he'd gone commando or snagged his boxers with his thumbs and done what she'd heard call a doubler.

His cock sprang out of its confines like a lure from a trap. She wasn't a greyhound and it wasn't a race. However, she could appreciate and drool over what she saw.

"Back to you." Braam toed off his trousers and stood with not one whit of self-consciousness as far as Debra could tell.

Probably had plenty of practice. It was a snide thought and not one she was proud of.

She bit her lip and put her hands behind her back to unclasp her bra. The hooks jammed and she fiddled with them, as she got hotter, for all the wrong reasons.

"Here, let me." Braam twirled her around so her back was facing him. Typically, the hooks slid out of the fasteners as if they'd never been stuck and the cups of her bra fell away from her body. He slipped the straps down over her elbows and her bra hung awkwardly over her ribs. Or where she thought her ribs should be. It was a few years since she'd felt them easily.

"Arms out." Braam gave one of her elbows a nudge, and Debra did as he'd asked. He took one, then the other strap over her hands and wrists and dropped her bra on top of his clothes.

"No, don't turn round, not yet." He drew her nearer, until his cock rubbed her ass through the lacy but not overly sexy undies she wore. How he managed to line it up, she didn't know and didn't much care, as long as he didn't discontinue his slow, sensual movements.

He stroked her nipples at the same time as he nuzzled the nape of her neck. Nipped her skin and pinched those rapidly hardening nubs.

Debra moaned and swayed backwards. *Ah shoot, like the heroine in whatever book he was talking about.* His cock pressed between the two round globes. Even through the lace that covered her, his pre-cum slicked her skin.

"These would be best off this time." Braam pushed the sides of her undies down her legs and Debra did a tiny shimmy to help them on their way.

"Oh, I like that. The hip swivel, boob jiggle is definitely guaranteed to get my cock harder and ready for you." The bite and suck on her neck created ripples of heat over her skin. "It won't show, I promise, not unless you're naked. Then it's all for me."

"Do I get to repay the favor?" Her voice was husky.

"Later. Much later." Braam lifted his head and held her breasts in her hands as at the same time he rubbed her nipples in his fingers. "I think we'd be more comfy in bed." He moved his hands to her hips and gave her a tiny shove. "Go on, honey, I'll bring the wine and the condoms."

Debra moved forward and couldn't believe how cold she felt once they weren't skin to skin.

The long, low whistle made her jump and she turned round.

"Your tattoo. It's the same as mine."

She nodded.

"And I reckon if I put my thigh next to your ass they'd be kissing tattoos."

"Novel." Debra climbed up on the bed. Similar to the one they'd spent time in the previous night, but somehow, here and surrounded by the knick-knacks she'd picked up on her travels, it seemed so much more intimate.

"No, tattoos." Braam put the glasses plus the bottle in a cooler onto the table beside him. "So maybe we'd better be kissing before they do, eh?"

He rolled over and pushed her legs apart. His cock nudged her clit and with a jolt Debra registered that he'd put the condom on without her noticing.

Her pussy contracted as Braam slipped one then two fingers into her essence-filled channel. It wasn't enough.

"Oh, so ready." He crooned the words as he added a third finger and played with her clit with his thumb. "*Are* you ready, love? I'm holding it together here by a thread and if you keep making those soft mewls and sexy moans, I'll lose it."

She hadn't even known she *was* making any noise. She wriggled and lifted her ass from the bed. "Mmm, more."

Braam grinned and leaned back on his ankles to put her legs over his shoulders.

Then he bent his head and licked her clit and pussy.

If he hadn't held her tight, Debra would have arched off the bed and hit the ceiling. Even so, she pushed into him with her mound and his breath skittered over her hot skin.

He seemed to understand her unspoken entreaty and scraped his teeth over her clit. That tiny action was enough for Debra to fall into a deep, hard, fast and explosive climax that made her scream and sob. Her body shook and she saw stars. Tiny silver dots danced in front of her eyes.

Without really knowing what she was doing, Debra groped for Braam's cock.

"In me, please. In me now."

He lifted his mouth, just for a second. His laugh was soft and triumphant before he dipped his head again and sucked her clit into his mouth.

The pleasure-pain sped through her and the final judders of her first climax morphed into the first ones of her next. Before she had time to sort what was which, Braam moved and his cock nudged the entrance to her channel.

He clenched her ass with his hands and put it exactly where she assumed he wanted it. At the right height for him to move in and out with ease.

Debra closed her eyes to concentrate on all the emotions that swirled through her. Then she opened them because she didn't want to miss seeing him as he loomed over her. Now he used his hands for balance. The muscles on his arms and in his neck stood out as Braam thrust into her and set up a steady rhythm of filling her and withdrawing almost to the tip of his dick. Then to repeat the process over and over again.

His eyes were closed and his breathing shallow as he pounded into her.

Debra reveled in the sense of rightness and clenched and unclenched her muscles to encourage him, to hold him and let him slide in and out.

Braam opened his eyes and focused on her face.

"Now." He roared the word and moved one hand to pinch her clit. As his climax overwhelmed him, his body shook and his breath came in short harsh pants.

It was enough for Debra to join him.

Chapter Five

Watching the woman you were more than half in love with sleep was an eye opener. She slept like she made love. With abandonment. One leg was out of the covers, the other tucked between his with her knee rather too close to his cock for comfort. She was stretched out on her left side, facing him and with her head on his chest. Braam liked that. One of her hands rested on his chest, holding onto the short hair sprinkled over his skin, and the other hand was wrapped around his cock.

Braam considered his options. As much as he was loath to leave her, he had no option. He needed to go back to his room, change and get downstairs before anyone saw where he'd appeared from and put two and two together correctly.

It was hard to lift her arm from his cock and try to wriggle backwards. Debra muttered something incoherent and her fingers in his chest hair tightened. Braam winced. He was partial to the dark fuzz that covered him.

"Love, I need to go." He tried to prize open Debra's fingers.

"Eh?" She opened her eyes, but it was obvious she hadn't woken up properly. "Wassup?"

"I have to go." He kissed her nose and she scrunched it up. "I still work here and I can't be seen to do the walk of shame. I need to check things before we go out."

"Mmm, I could check things for you." Debra slid down his body, let her knee stroke his balls, and kissed his cock.

"I think maybe you could." All thoughts of an early getaway fled out of his head, as his half erect cock indicated it wanted to play. "Check away."

There was a whirring noise as Debra flicked the switch to open the blinds a few inches and allowed the dim dawn light to illuminate the room.

"Well, let me see." She leaned on her elbows. "Two nipples still there." She kissed each in turn and let her teeth close around them very gently. Braam let his breath out in one long hiss. It was damned erotic.

"Oh, good," he said weakly. "That's a relief. Anything else to report?"

She lifted her head. "Shh, don't interrupt or I'll forget where I've got to and have to start again."

"A, b, c, d, e, me, you, let us see," he recited.

Debra moved her elbow back and dug into in his stomach.

"Ooft."

"Now you've put me off," she said and sniggered.

"Oh, I don't think so." Braam rolled over and took her with him. "But, in case, shall I take over?"

She blew over his chest. "Be my guest."

"Oh, I intend to. Do you have room for a little one?" He pressed his not so little cock against her pussy.

Debra giggled. "Not for a little one, no. But for this one..." She wriggled so his cock rubbed over her slit." Oh, yes."

Being Debra's guest took much longer than either of them had anticipated.

Braam did the walk of shame, or to be accurate the jog of shame, with one eye open for staff and the other for any guest who would wonder why he looked like he'd been pulled through a hedge backward.

He had gotten half-dressed before Deb had bet him double or quits. He'd lost.

So an hour and a half later than he meant to, he went into his room and had yet another cold shower. And couldn't have cared less. He'd left her sated and rumpled in the middle of a bomb site laughingly known as a bed and elicited a promise that she'd be ready in an hour. That gave him little time to change, but, he reasoned, it also gave the in-house staff less time to panic and ask for help over things they were well able to cope with.

When he left the hotel, he checked his phone. The most welcome message was on it.

Ohh for a loser (lol) you pay your forfeits beautifully. See you next to the litter, cum, recyclables, collection bin (eeuk).

It was Braam's turn to roll his eyes and snigger. The long metal bins for all the detritus of the streets were marked like that and the cum bit had made him snigger more than once.

As he approached the corner where they had arranged to meet, he saw Debra leaning on a lamp post. He walked up to her unnoticed and goosed her. She screeched like a banshee and swung round with her fingers straight and taut. Braam managed to evade the vicious jab by a millimeter. Her shriek and her "You fucking idiot" were so loud that several people turned to look at them. Braam had the unnerving suspicion that he was about to become a statistic in Hong Kong's citizens' arrests for this month when Debra flung her arms around him.

"You lug, you great big eejit. God, I love you, but you scared the bejeezus out of me."

He grinned and swung her round in a circle, unheeding of the passers-by. "Always expect the unexpected. And I didn't expect that. Any of it. Especially the love bit."

Her eyes widened. "Put me down, Braam. We're too old for this malarkey. And love is a…a generic word."

"Hmm, if you say so." He'd let it go for now, but he intended to quiz her when they were on their walk. When she couldn't evade him. "Let's go." He hitched his backpack over his shoulder, went to take hers from her. The glint in her eye stopped him.

"Thank you."

Those two words almost stopped him in his tracks. "What for, hon?"

She shrugged and slipped her hand into his. "Oh, I don't know. Nothing. Everything. For not pushing anything." She sniggered. "Well, not quite anything. I'm glad something got pushed." She looked toward his cock and back up to his face. "And for being the gentleman and accepting I can carry my own bag."

He pondered her words as they headed toward the MTR. Had he accepted everything? Well, no, not all of it, but he was prepared to bide his time and give her some leeway. But not in everything. He took two Oyster cards out of his pocket. The public transport prepaid tickets were a godsend and saved lots of queuing.

He handed one to Debra and waited for the argument. There wasn't one. She took it with a smile and a murmured word of thanks and followed him down to the platform.

* * * *

"So, tell me a bit about yourself." Braam stretched his legs out as best he could. The seats on the ferry might have a bit more padding than when he was a child, but he was sure that the legroom had shrunk. Of course, he was several feet taller than when his parents had brought him to walk the island all those years ago.

"Show and tell time?" Debra sat sideways on hers with her back to the window. The sun's rays bounced off the waves of the harbor and created a halo around her head. Braam wasn't sure that angelic was the label he'd put to her. Feisty, adventurous, sexy, hot as hell and his.

Mine? Where had that come from? Nevertheless, he accepted he meant it.

"Well, I reckon we've done a fair bit of showing already," Braam said and she punched his shoulder. He winced theatrically and rubbed where her fist had landed. It didn't hurt. He'd have to show her how to make a proper fist.

"Below the belt, Van Meister."

"Oh, yes, a lot of showing there."

She chuckled. A deep-throated, sexy roar that made several people turn and stare at them. "Oh, how true. Okay, so do we toss for first dibs?"

Braam raised one eyebrow. Debra rolled her eyes.

"Give over with the double entendre making, or we'll get thrown off for gross indecent thinking." She swiveled to sit straight on the seat as the ferry shuddered and began to move. "Okay, well, Debra Anne Scotburn, nee Robinson. You know how old I am. Widowed five years ago. Born and brought up in Scotland, both parents Scottish. Left school and spent a year visiting friends and relatives all around the world. We didn't call it a gap year then. Met Don in my first week of uni."

"Lecturer?"

Debra shook her head. "Nope, he was fixing the wiring in my halls of residence. There was this big redheaded hunk up a ladder and his ass was at eye level. I, er, tripped and had to grab the ladder so I didn't fall over." She winked.

"Good one. And?"

"We chatted, we fell in love and got married six months later. I took a year out when I found I was pregnant with my twins. The rest is history. We were a conventional normal family until Don was diagnosed with cancer and died within three months. I floundered until the kids said I needed to move on. And I thought, yeah, they're right. Don, bless him, was a real home bird, so we didn't travel. This was my chance. I don't think it was quite what the kids had in mind."

Braam made up his mind he was with the kids on that one. Sexist though it might be. She seemed too small and too innocent to roam the world alone. He allowed himself a mental smile. Maybe innocent wasn't the right word.

"Your turn. Ohhh, look." She pointed to the hillside they were passing. A tiny temple showed up between the thickly wooded slopes. "Isn't it cute? Oh, I love Hong Kong."

"Yep, my home. Okay." He forestalled her next comment. "I know, my turn. Right, so Abraham Van Meister, aged thirty-two and a big bit."

She chuckled, and he grinned. "Single because I've never met anyone I wanted to stay with." He paused and took hold of Debra's hand. "Until now." He continued talking before she could comment. He didn't want to hear her say he was talking crap or a bad risk or something. "I guess you could say I'm a mongrel. Grandparents, let me see. One Chinese, one Portuguese, one Dutch, one English. So my dad is Dutch English and Mum Chinese Portuguese. I was born in England, then we lived in Macau for a while when I was little. Moved to Hong Kong when I was ten and been here ever since. Apart from university in England and when I get sent to wherever my bosses need me. I was going to take you to see my home, but I reckoned we needed a good old touristy day. Home will keep. Look, that's where we're heading for." He leaned toward Debra and pointed ahead. Her scent teased him once more.

The tiny fishing village was getting bigger as the ferry drew nearer. People gathered their belongings together as the boat commenced its maneuver into the dock. Braam hefted his backpack off the floor.

"That looks heavy," Debra commented as they joined the queue to disembark.

"I have cold drinks and snacks in it. I thought we'd eat once we've walked the trail and if the boy who sells ice creams at the top isn't there, we'll be glad of them. Actually, we'll be glad of them anyway. It's going to be humid."

The sun was high and hazy and as they left the air-conditioned ferry cabin, the heat hit them in waves. Debra untucked her T-shirt from the waistband of her cut-offs. "Blimey, you aren't wrong. Is it always like this so early in the year?"

Braam shook his head as he took her hand and turned her away from the single village street lined with fish restaurants and tiny food shops. The smell of spices and hot, used fat followed them. "Nope, it's come early. And you never get used to it, not totally. You thank the Lord for air con and do everything whilst it's cooler. That's why we're out and about so early."

They walked past a children's play park and a map of the island. Debra stopped to look at the map.

"It says that we want to go the other way." She traced the trail with her finger.

"We do," Braam agreed amiably. After I've shown you something. Not the 'you show me yours and I'll show you mine' either."

Debra chuckled. "Maybe not, not here. Oh my goodness, look at that." She waved their joint hands toward a ramshackle row of shacks. "Are they still used for people to eat in? Really?"

"They sure are. After all, who wouldn't want to eat in Jonnies, the Best Seafood Restaurant Ever, or the Best Peking Duck outside Peking Sunshine Café?"

"Hmm, if you don't fall through the floor, or get eaten by something." Debra wrinkled her nose. "Still, looks can be deceiving, I guess. One of the best meals I ever had was in a tiny wooden hut over a lagoon in South Africa. You could see through the cracks in the floor to the water and I swear they used to fish through them to catch the oysters. And they were the best oysters I've ever tasted."

"Knysna?"

She looked surprised. "Yes, have you been there?"

"Oh, have I ever. It was my getaway from the pressure of the job place when I worked in South Africa a few years ago. Damn shame when they modernized it. It's not even there now. The rent went up so much, they pulled it down, along with a few other ramshackle but brilliant restaurants and bars. Modernizing and not in a good way."

Debra had to agree with him. Modernization wasn't always the way to go, although she thought the row of wooden shacks they'd passed a few moments earlier would benefit from some.

The track climbed the side of the hill away from the water. Debra wondered where on earth they were going. If she'd read the map correctly, they'd have to retrace their tracks to find the path over the hills to the other, larger fishing village where they could catch another ferry back to Central. No wonder they'd had an early start. It wasn't solely because of the humidity. Braam had a plan.

Hand in hand, they walked along companionably until Braam turned off the track onto a tiny dirt trail that twisted and turned around the scrubby bushes and trees as it made its way downhill.

"I'll go first. Watch your step, it's a bit uneven. Our destination is a few minutes away at most. We used to come here almost every week when I was growing up. It was always deserted apart from one old guy fishing off the rocks. I never ever saw him catch anything. Here we are."

The track became sandier and Debra strode out, only to stub her toe on a half-hidden stone

"Dammit, ouch. These damn pebbles stick up like olives in a pizza. I hate olives."

Braam turned and kissed her nose. "Do you need kissing better?'

Debra shuddered theatrically. "Eugh, no thank you. It was my toe. I hope to goodness toe sucking isn't one of your fetishes? Because if it is, you're out of luck. Like I said before, my feet are a no go zone."

"You're safe, that's not on my list. Ear sucking, nipple sucking, clit sucking? Oh, yes, but I've never made it low enough to want to toe suck. I get waylaid at the c —"

"Yes, well, oh, good, oh grief." Debra was sure her cheeks matched the color of her underwear. Her best worn in the pool and not suffered underwear. Not that he could see it, thankfully.

Braam stood to one side and waved his arm. "Voilà."

In front of them the view changed to one of blue sky and sunlit sea.

The tiny cove was enchanting. Across the water, Debra could see land. Tree-covered hills dotted with houses and, perhaps, a road, where vehicles shone as the sun reflected off them.

"Where's that?" She pointed across the water.

Braam came up behind her and put his arms around her. His hands rested on the swells of her breasts. "That's Hong Kong Island. That way —" he lifted one arm and pointed —"is Aberdeen and the typhoon shelter. Over there is Stanley. Good view, eh?" He put his arm back around her and his finger brushed her nipple before settling nearby.

Just an inch across please. Debra leaned back into his embrace and wriggled so his finger slipped and tightened over her nipple. It hardened and peaked the soft material that covered it.

"Oh, someone's pleased to have attention." Braam kissed the nape of her neck. She shivered. He did that so well. Deb bent her head to give him better access.

There was a clatter of pebbles and they both looked up. Debra noticed and felt that Braam didn't move his arms more than the inch needed for them not to be making out in public.

An old man emerged from the track they had used. He had on an incongruous tartan tammy, a fishing rod over one shoulder and a bucket in his hand. He grinned, showing three blackened teeth, then bowed his head and said something.

Braam answered him. His voice rose at the end of his speech, so Debra judged that he had asked the older man a question.

The man cackled and spat expertly into the bushes. Debra averted her head. Even though spitting was now illegal in Hong Kong, she doubted that many people were prosecuted on Lamma, especially not on a beach. It was highly unlikely that a policeman was going to pop up from behind a bush.

The man spoke again and Braam chuckled and waved. Debra looked at him.

"Wow, you actually do speak the lingo." Deb fluttered her eyelashes. "You *are* clever."

"Yeah, of course. How else would I order dim sum from the street vendor? Hold on." The older man was speaking once more. Braam responded and the guy grunted, gave his gappy grin and walked down the beach.

"He said he never catches anything. He comes down when his wife has her sisters over for lunch. He needs the peace."

"Is it the same guy as when you were a kid?"

Braam smiled. "I'd guess not, he'd be about ninety now. But who knows? Ah well, bang goes my chance of seducing you here. I was going to add to my memory bank. Shall we go? We need to face the gauntlet of all the hustlers outside the restaurants before we can get onto the trail."

Debra nodded, more disappointed than she would have imagined. His brief almost caress had set her pulse racing and her imagination into overdrive. She followed him back through the trees to the main track.

* * * *

He was correct about the hustling. Debra was glad she had Braam for protection. Although most people took a polite no for an answer, some were more persistent. When one guy grabbed Debra's arm, Braam snarled and gave the man such a mouthful that he took a step backwards and almost hit his chest with his head as he said something in a most apologetic tone. No one else bothered them after that.

Did the restaurateurs and shopkeepers have some sort of semaphore or code that said don't mess with this man?

"What did you say to him?" Debra asked curiously. "He went pale."

"I threatened him with my uncle. He has the same name as a bit of a bad 'un in Macao. It works every time. Though Uncle Abilio wouldn't hurt a fly. He's a scientist and rarely steps out of his bubble."

"I love it. Braam, how many languages *do* you speak?"

"Um, well, as opposed to the 'hello', 'please', 'thank you', 'goodbye', 'where's the loo'? and 'can I have the bill please'? variety? Mandarin, Cantonese, Portuguese, Dutch and English."

She blinked. "Blimey, that makes my schoolgirl French pathetic."

"Maybe your talents run in a different direction?" He raised one eyebrow and leered.

She sniggered. "Yeah. Cross stitch. I'm a dab hand at jabbing with a needle."

He put his hands over his cock.

She shook her head. "Am I likely to need to... No, don't answer that. Oh, look." She moved faster toward a shop front a few yards away then stopped.

Braam turned to look at her with a quizzical expression. "What?"

"Them." She gestured toward a stall. "I want those."

"You want? Cheap here." The stallholder had caught the word 'want'.

"The kids' chopsticks?" Braam asked her incredulously. "With the cartoon plasticy thing holding them together? Why? Oh, duh, you're present buying."

"Well, yes and no. It is a present, but it's for me and do not laugh," Debra said. She knew she sounded defensive. "I need them all right? I can*not* use proper chopsticks to save myself. Okay, I can't use these in public, but at least I can give myself the illusion of eating Chinese food the Chinese way when I'm alone." She shut up as Braam embarked on the expected haggling with the shopkeeper. At least she assumed that was what he was doing. There was a lot of head shaking and fingers held in the air, until finally he and the shopkeeper shook hands.

"Choose your color, love. Do you want the slimy green whatever it is or the pink star?"

"The star, of course, thank you. Hold on, I need to get my money out." Debra swung her shoulder bag around.

Braam put his hand on her bag and stopped her. "My treat. All ten Hong Kong dollars of it. Around seventy odd of your pence. I'm a cheapskate." He handed a note to the shopkeeper and took his change and the chopsticks in a neat purple net bag. It almost didn't clash with the fastening of the chopsticks.

Debra stood on tiptoe to kiss him. As soon as her lips touched his, she felt the familiar clit tingling, muscle clenching sensations that she experienced every time they touched. Damned if he didn't send her bones to jelly and make her mouth water. The brief hard clench of her ass as he returned the kiss made her moan. She moaned again as his grip lessened and he ended the kiss and the ass-hold.

"You, my love, will have us arrested if we're not careful." Braam was breathing heavily as he ran his hand through his short hair. "One touch and I forget where we are. We could be in the middle of a crowd at a major sporting event and I'd still lose track of anything but you."

Awww. There was no answer, except, "Thank you, I feel the same."

"Good, but we need to curb our enthusiasm in public. Right, shall we get a move on? I've earmarked a place for snacks and drinks, but we need to walk a bit. Is that all right with you?"

"Oh, yes." They linked hands again and left the shops, restaurants and houses behind to climb the steep track out of the village. Debra soon found she was puffing. Okay, she didn't like exercise per se, but she liked walking and did a lot of it. This was something else. Sweat dripped down her back and between her boobs. She'd be getting the adult equivalent of nappy rash between them, not on her butt if she wasn't careful. She tried to wipe her cleavage surreptitiously and stole a mutinous look at Braam. He, of course, looked as if he was strolling along the promenade of stars on Kowloon waterfront and ready to see if his handprint matched Jackie Chan's or Bruce Li's.

"What?" Braam handed her a bottle of ice-cold water. "You were muttering."

Debra took a long swig before she answered. If she wasn't so thirsty, she'd pour half the water over her head to cool herself off and the other half over Braam just because.

"Wondering how, if I bashed you over the head, I'd get back to Central. How on earth can they say this is a stroll?"

"To be honest, I don't think anyone says that," Braam pointed out. "It says it's a walk over the hills."

"Hm, it says around four kilometers and about an hour. We've been going for at least three." *Sheesh, I sound a right mardy bitch, but seriously, this is tough.* Debra hated feeling like that. All whiney, poor me pathos.

"On this track, twenty minutes. Do you want to go back? We can get a ferry where we landed."

He sounded so concerned that Debra's bad mood dissipated like the early morning mist over the Peak. She had to hope it didn't roll back in like it did over the Peak.

"No, I'm fine, honestly." She hugged him then drank some more water. "I'm hot and bothered for all the wrong reasons. I want to go on. I was having a moment. A pissy moment." She snapped the water bottle lid closed. "Sorry. All okay now."

"Honey, I was pushing you. We'll take it steady now. Are you up for a tiny detour? No more than ten minutes each way and somewhere to sit and nibble."

Nibble what? "Of course I am. Lead on, MacDuff, or should I say, Van M.?"

Braam tapped the tip of her nose with his little finger. A for no reason but friendly gesture as far as Debra could tell. Whatever, it made her go all tingly inside.

"Either will do. Do you want me to take your bag?"

"Nope, I've pulled up my big girl panties and I'm fine." Debra put her holdall over her shoulder.

"Damn, I was hoping you were in those interesting scraps of lace I glimpsed in the pool. Mind your step. This bit's narrow and the steps are slippery. Let me go ahead. Then, if you slip you'll fall on me, not down the hill."

How could she concentrate on steps when he made a statement like that?

She waited until the path became reasonably level. "I am."

Braam stopped dead and she bumped into him. He turned round to look at her. "You are what?"

Debra ran her tongue round her lips very slowly and smiled. She made her voice as deep and sultry as she knew how. "In those interesting scraps of lace you glimpsed."

He blinked and swallowed. His Adam's apple moved convulsively. "Woman," he said hoarsely. "You'll be the death of me. Come on." He grabbed her hand and turned along a side track.

What is it with him and wee side trails?

"Shut your eyes."

"Pardon?"

He grinned. "Shut your eyes, please, love, and trust me."

When he put it like that, Debra couldn't even think of refusing him.

She closed her eyes and felt him lead her forward. There was a rustling noise. "Stand still a sec." He let her go.

Debra kept her eyes shut and strained to hear anything. What if it was a cruel joke and he left her? What if...? She didn't get onto any worse a scenario before Braam took hold of her around her waist. Even with her eyes shut, she knew it was him. Strange how she'd gotten to know his touch and recognized his scent.

"Okay, now let me help you sit down." His arm pressed her down, and Debra put her arms out to help. She felt a soft blanket or some such thing under her hands and let herself be seated.

"Now open your eyes."

Debra did as he'd bid and gasped. Spread out in front of them was a vista even better than the one from his childhood picnic beach. The little clearing amongst the bushes was perhaps a hundred feet above the waves. And totally secluded. As far as she could tell, no one walking down the track could see them.

"Private and you have to know it's here and how to find it." It seemed Braam was reading her mind once more.

"How do you do that?" Debra leaned back on her arms and watched a couple of sailing dinghies and several container ships cross from one side of the view to the other.

"Do what?" Braam sat down next to her and undid his backpack."

"Read my mind."

He chuckled and intoned in a deep, sepulchral voice, "It is a gift given solely to a chosen few."

"Well, one of the chosen few. What am I thinking now?"

"You need to pee and then eat. If you go behind those bushes, it's private and you'll not be in danger of falling down the cliff."

She blushed. *Damn him, he was right.*

"Thank you." Debra headed for the indicated bushes. She hoped they were far enough away from where Braam waited for her not to have to whistle. She cleared her throat and tried an off-key trill of *New York, New York.*

A few minutes later she brushed past the last bush and re-entered the clearing. Braam looked up from the rug. Behind it, he'd set out a tablecloth, plastic wine glasses and a Thermos.

"All better?"

"Ssh, it's embarrassing." Debra sat down on the blanket and watched him rummage in his backpack.

"Not at all. I went thataway." Braam pointed behind him. "And I whistled." He poured two glasses of wine and set them on a handy flat stone. It made a perfect table.

"What did you whistle?" Debra asked. "I did *New York, New York.*"

"Oh, classy lady. I was much more mundane. I tried *Bring Me Sunshine.*" The thought of the both of them whistling away to cover the sound of them peeing in the bushes made Debra giggle. Braam stared and his shoulders heaved as he cracked up.

"What a pair."

Debra nodded. "It was a bit, er, delicate, I guess. Still it's one way to get to know each other better. We, er, know each other's taste in music for moments." She burst out laughing again.

Braam raised his eyebrows. "We know each other's tastes in more than that." He rolled sideways across the blanket and tugged Debra by the ankle until she was stretched out flat on her back. Then Braam pulled her on top of him. "I know," he said softly as he ran his fingers through her hair. "Like I know you make such sexy little purrs when I kiss you here." He kissed the soft skin beneath her ear. "And here makes you wriggle and moan." This time it was the nape of her neck. "Ohh and here makes you wet and needy and hot, hot, hot." He rolled them over so she was beneath him and ran his fingers over her cheek, across her chest and dipped it into the valley between her breasts. His grin was wicked as he slid his hand under the lacy cup of her bras and nipped her nipple. "And you groan, yes, like that. Groan for me, love, sigh your arousal. Show me what I do to you. Close your eyes, let go and enjoy my touch. Please, love."

He whispered his words in her ear. Her eyelids closed and she was cocooned in a world of words and touch and warmth. His voice caressed her. Soft, low, arousing and full of desire. "Let me touch you here." He moved the hand he wasn't using to send a sharp stab of sweet excitement from her nipple to her clit and unsnapped the button at the waistband of her cut-offs.

Debra couldn't have formed a coherent thought if her life depended on it. His scent filled her senses, his touch sent her body into a spiraling vortex of light and heat and her super-sensitive skin sang with each touch he gave her.

When he put two fingers into her wet vagina, she screamed.

Braam swallowed it with a kiss. His fingers teased and caressed her channel and his thumb pressed on her clit. Rainbows danced across the inside of her eyelids. Every fiber of her soul concentrated on Braam and his words and actions.

"Come for me, love." His hand moved faster, in and out of her pussy, swirling around her clit, as he nipped, rubbed and teased her. Then he kissed her throat. "Fly for us." He whispered the words in her ear. It was the 'us' that did it. Debra turned her head into his chest and flew.

Chapter Six

To see Debra splinter and come apart in his arms was more satisfying than Braam had ever imagined. Each time she put her trust in him and let herself feel, Braam sank further under her spell.

Her breath came in tiny hitching sobs and her pulse raced so fast it was a perfect beat for a workout. With her face buried against his chest, even through his T-shirt her breath touched his skin with a warmth and caress solely for him. More content than he'd been for months, Braam held Debra in his arms, stroked her hair and whispered nonsense to her. Eventually she gave something between a shiver and a shudder and sniffed.

Braam took out a tissue from his pocket. "Blow."

Debra gave a watery laugh. "Bully." She took the tissue. "Thank you."

"You're welcome. Blow."

The silly conversation was the beginning of a chatty, companionable half hour. Debra accepted a glass of wine and snuck a glance or three in the direction of Braam's groin. He glanced down to where she looked.

The hard ridge of his cock was clearly outlined under the cargo shorts he wore and he grinned ruefully.

"Seems to be a usual state of affairs when I get close to you. It's somewhat unusual for me and I'm all over thrilled. Except when I'm in a meeting and even thinking of us gets me like this. Then I'm glad of a table to sit at or a large file to put in my lap."

"Aw, poor thing." Debra rested on one elbow and smiled at him. The scents and perfumes of the shrubs and flowers filled the air and vied with her subtle scent.

He resolved there and then he would never forget this place and this moment in time. Stretched out in the sunshine opposite Debra and simply enjoying it. No timetable, no lists, got to do, watch the clock, hurry up. Just there that moment. "I can't do anything in a meeting, but I think I have a solution for the here and now."

Debra moved to settle in a position the mirror of his own. "Oh, do you? What's that then?"

"Well..." Braam wriggled closer. "You see... Oh, bugger."

"Oh, shit."

Big fat raindrops fell out of the sky and rapidly increased in frequency. Braam stood up and pulled Debra to her feet. Even though the rain was warm, Debra shivered. Braam stamped down on his own chill. Talk about cooling your ardor.

"Quick, grab the tablecloth and put it on the ground between those two bushes. This rug has a waterproof cover and I'll flip it to make a makeshift cover. We don't have time to get anywhere undercover. It's only a shower and will soon pass, but it'll be heavy."

She could vouchsafe for that. As Debra lifted the tablecloth from the grass, her top was already damp. Much longer and she'd be soaked. She walked across the now slippery surface to the place Braam had indicated. By some quirk of nature the bushes had almost closed the gap between then, but left a space beneath, practically big enough for two people as long as they were friendly.

Under their branches the ground was still fairly dry. She spread the tablecloth over the grass and wriggled backwards to help Braam.

"Stay there, there's no point in us both getting soaked." Braam maneuvered the blanket onto the top of the shrubs and somehow fastened it. Inside the tiny shelter, the air seemed warmer and the atmosphere intimate. Braam thrust his T-shirt at Debra and went back to their picnic spot to gather the wine and glasses, her holdall and his backpack. He passed her everything he'd picked up and backed into the shelter.

Raindrops glistened in his hair and water ran down his chest. The sea was hidden behind clouds and Debra judged the temperature had dropped a good few degrees.

"Brr, damned storms. At least it'll soon pass over and we can head for the village." Braam shook his head and water flew everywhere. Debra gasped and shivered as the cold liquid sprinkled over her. "Oh, shit, sorry. Hold on, let me get my jumper out of my pack for you to put on."

She shook her head. "No need, I've got a fleece in mine. You need yours anyway." Debra touched his shoulder. "Hell's bells, Braam, you're freezing. Get dry and warm. I wish we had coffee, but seriously I never even thought about that. Not here at this time of the year."

Braam picked up his T-shirt and pulled it on. "This'll help. And so will this." He rummaged in his backpack and took out a dark gray sweatshirt. "Shove over a sec."

Debra watched as he spread the sweatshirt where she'd sat. With a grin, she turned and knelt over her holdall and pulled out one almost identical. "Snap. Shove over a sec." She pushed him, so he did as she'd asked and set her own sweatshirt next to his. "What next? Ah I know." Debra opened the tiny zipped pocket in lining and took out a foil packet. "This. I bet we could warm each other somehow. Especially if we use everything we have available to us."

Braam lay back and put his hands under his head and kept his legs bent at the knees. It didn't look that comfortable. "I do like a lady who thinks of everything. I think I'll leave it up to you to decide what happens next." He seemed totally at ease with his decision.

Debra knelt backward onto her ankles and tilted her head to one side. "Maybe if you took your shorts off you could use them as a pillow instead of your hands," she said. "Because I have a much better job for your hands later."

He looked at her, considering. "You do it."

It wasn't a suggestion. Debra took it to mean either she did as he said or nothing else would happen. She didn't want that.

The space they were in was tiny. If Braam stretched out properly, he'd be lucky to keep his feet dry. The rain still came down and splattered off the branches and blanket, creating soft sounds of life-giving water. Debra took a deep breath to take in the scents of damp earth and damp man. Different but both oh so good.

The intimate area was going to create some interesting strategies. Debra kicked off her shoes. The last thing she wanted was to accidentally kick him, but at least if her feet were bare it shouldn't hurt as much. She didn't tell him how clumsy she was reckoned to be. She shuffled on her knees until she was a hair's breadth away from Braam and undid the belt that presumably held his shorts up. He moved one hand and stroked her neck. It seemed to be a favorite thing of his to do, to touch her like that. Debra realized it was fast becoming one of her favorites as well.

"If you do that, you'll distract me and I'll forget what I'm supposed to be doing," she said.

"No you won't. It'll concentrate your mind."

True.

"No, I won't." She repeated his words. "It will concentrate my mind. See? Concentrated." She tugged the zip until it was wide open. "Lift your arse so I can complete my task."

Braam laughed and grunted as he lifted his rear. "This is not easy without any leverage."

"Ah, well, practice makes perfect." Debra pulled the shorts over Braam's legs and folded them carefully. "Here you are. Your pillow, m'lord."

He bent his head in a parody of a bow. "Well, thank you kindly. May I ask what next?"

"This." Debra hooked her fingers in the elastic waistband of his boxers and pulled them downward. As they snagged on his erect cock, she paused. "Oh, my, what now. I seem to have a problem." She let her hands brush the sides of his dick and slowly slid them up and down.

"I'm sure you are incredibly good at problem solving." His cock swayed within her touch

Debra used one thumb and forefinger to circle it.

"Ah, oh, yes, that sure is a great start."

Braam sat up suddenly. "Now I think I'll help us along." He lifted her hands out of his boxers, shucked them himself, and pulled his T-shirt off so swiftly Debra hardly had time to blink. Then Braam lifted her top over her shoulders and put her into the space he'd so recently occupied. Her top had a built-in bra and his soft, triumphant laugh was music to her ears.

The tablecloth was warm under her back, as Braam lifted her head and gave her the makeshift pillow to rest on.

The kiss to her nipple was short, sharp and oh so sweet. That part of her skin rapidly became hotter than the rest of her. The state of affairs changed within seconds as Braam took off her cut-offs and pressed a heated kiss over the lace that covered her pussy.

"Such a sexy, teasing arousing sight. That beautiful pussy hidden in such an enticing way."

The whispered words made every penny she'd spent in the exclusive lingerie boutique worthwhile. The way he drew the lacy undies over her pussy and ass and down her legs, was almost reverential and the tiny kisses he followed in the path of the lace both tickled and made her squirm in arousal. Her pussy was damp and her vagina muscles were practicing their 'let me hold you, let me play with you, come into me' routine.

Braam spread her legs and settled between them. If it were still raining, he'd have a wet lower half.

When he lowered his head and licked and sucked her clit and pussy, Debra was damned sure she was wet as well.

He tugged her hard nub into his mouth and gently scraped his teeth over the skin. Debra arched into his mouth. "Oh, shit, I'll come again and I want to come with you inside me."

Braam lifted his head.

Damn, he didn't have to move so fast.

"Oh, I think you can manage to come now *and* when I'm in you. Look." He bent his head again and circled his tongue around the entrance to her channel. He pushed the tip of his tongue inside and bit the soft skin at the entrance.

Debra screamed and moved her head from side to side, to catch and hold that indefinable something that was just out of reach. Then she found it. Her movements increased. It was mind blowing and she couldn't have stopped her climax if she'd tried. She didn't try. Waves and waves of heat flowed through her.

"Now, for goodness' sake. Come in me now."

"Oh, yes."

Stings and tingles caressed and teased her skin as he plunged into her. Braam set up a fast and furious rhythm and Debra met him thrust for thrust. Each push, each nudge and every grunt she heard made her heart swell and its beat increase. He bent his head and bit her nipple before laving it with his tongue. The pain was swift and sent an immediate line of heat to her clit.

Her mind went blank. Coherent thought disappeared as she rode the waves of ecstasy.

How long she was in the throes of her arousal, Debra had no idea. When she finally stopped shuddering and opened her eyes, her head was on Braam's chest, which she noted with satisfaction was heaving like a tugboat in a gale.

"Whew." *What an insipid exclamation for something so out of the world.* Sadly her tired brain couldn't come up with anything less mundane.

"Yeah." As ever, Braam played with her hair and stroked her cheek and throat.

She'd have to ask him if in the lieu of worshiping toes, he had a fetish about her head instead. *Later.*

"You complete me, Deb. I can't think of any other way to say it."

Those simple words made her swell up and sniff. "Oh, my. And you me."

He cuddled her closer. "Just as well." He was silent for a moment and Debra was content to stay as they were. "Listen, it's stopped raining. We'd better make a move before the next storm rolls in. There might not be another convenient place to shelter and we don't want to get all soaked and have a damp ferry ride back."

Debra giggled as she reluctantly moved off his chest and sat up. She looked around and found her top.

"Oh, that's okay. I have a raincoat."

Braam stared at her. "You do? That's good because so do I. Great minds and all that."

It seemed they were in harmony in more ways than one.

* * * *

Once Braam had dismantled the makeshift shelter and packed everything away, it took next to no time to regain the track and continue on their way.

Once more the sun was out and the humidity hit them hard.

"I wish that I'd bought one of those fans you put round you forehead." Debra waved her hand in front of her face like a fan. "And I wish we could have left our wee hidey hole as it was." She spoke in a wishful tone. "You know, as a perpetual reminder of a fantastic rainstorm."

"And have every chancing it youth of Lamma getting up to God knows what there?" Braam was more prosaic. "As it is, no one goes there because it's off the beaten track and there are easier, more comfortable places for them to make out. Best to leave it as is. Then when we're old and gray we can find it again and relive our memories."

Debra laughed, even though her pulse jumped. Was it a good sign? An omen he was talking about when they were old? Or was it a generalization? She wasn't going to ask.

"With our Zimmers and saying things aren't like they were in our younger days?"

"Probably. Look, here's the lad with the ice lollies. Want one?"

The lollies were eaten as they walked down the hill. The youth, who couldn't have been more than fifteen, had entreated them to buy two each, as he said the rain had made business slow. Braam had laughingly declined, but nevertheless Debra was sure Braam had paid over the going rate.

He denied it as they exchanged bites. Debra had asked for lime, Braam had gone for lemon.

"I paid what they were worth," he said. "No more, no less. Look." He pointed down the track to where a sliver of sand showed. "If we cross that and get into the village proper, there's a plethora of restaurants to try. But..." He paused. "Do you trust me?"

Debra wasn't sure why—or what exactly—he was asking. "Of course. Well, unless you're going to tell me you have a wife and six kids or you have a bridge to sell me. Why?"

"None of those." He flicked her nose with his finger. "It's six wives and one kid and seven bridges."

"Oh, no problem then. What's up?"

"I know a great restaurant, but it's Indian food. Moz does a great mutton curry to friends. What do you say?"

Debra swore she salivated. Mutton curry. Oh, joy.

"I say, yes please, please."

"Sorted. Five minutes, come on."

Braam dragged her — there was no other word for it — past tourist shops, stalls selling fast foods and the odd leaflet peddler until they turned off the main street and into a square next to the water.

"Here." He pushed open a door painted in a myriad of colors and Debra smelled heaven.

"Hey, Moz, can you feed two weary walkers?" Braam dragged her inside. "Outside, so I can romance my lady with sweet nothings and seduce her with your food?" Braam hugged the tall Indian who had him in a death grip.

"Moz, man, don't kill me. What would my lady do then?"

Moz guffawed. It was a sound Deb hadn't heard for ages. A mix of the braying of a donkey and the squeal of a pig whose feed had been removed.

"Come to me, of course." He released Braam who winced and rubbed his chest. Debra wasn't entirely sure the gesture was theatrical. "Hello, Braam's lady. You are welcome here. Um, I hope you like curry?"

"Love it."

Moz swept her into his arms and bent her backward. It was so theatrical and so stupid Debra giggled.

He straightened and thrust her into Braam's arms. "Here, you have her. She doesn't appreciate me."

"And Sukhjinder wouldn't appreciate you molesting my woman."

Moz spread his hands out. "So true, and as she is in the kitchen behind several Karahi, here is your lady. Unmolested. The table on the left is for you." He waved toward the terrace. "It is under the cover if it's needed."

Debra looked at the sky as a young girl escorted them to their table. If she were a betting woman, she'd say it was odds on the cover would be needed. The sky was a sullen amber color and the hills looked dark and menacing.

All of a sudden she was glad they'd come down from the hill when they had and not purely because she was hungry.

Braam held her chair out for her and made sure he was back onto the outside. A nasty little wind had sprung up and teased the tablecloths. Moz bustled around with weights and table securers.

Braam gestured toward him. "He knows something we don't."

As if the words were a key, the heavens opened and within seconds the waiters sprang into action. Rain bounced like ping pong balls across the concrete square. The side curtains were rolled down and secured and the water was kept out.

Debra had wondered why the tables and chairs were raised up on pallets. Now she knew. Under them the water created streams as it rushed though the courtyard and to the harbor.

On the other side of the square, like a beautifully choreographed corps de ballet, the stallholders rolled large sheets of plastic over their wares then retreated under them to chat and smoke.

It was obviously well-practiced and a break from the mundane. The few tourists not sensible enough to take shelter splashed their way to the ferry terminus and those that had tried to seek shelter at Moz's were soon disappointed by the lack of tables. It wasn't over large.

Moz bustled toward their table with a carafe of wine, two glasses and a tray of poppadums and accompaniments. Debra looked at Braam. She didn't remember ordering anything

"Moz knows my tastes," Braam said when his friend had rushed away to tell yet more people there was no space. "I said we'd have whatever he decided on, because otherwise goodness knows when we'd eat. He's a bit busy."

That was the understatement of the century. Moz and his waiters rushed around like dervishes and served, cleared, chatted and Debra determined, generally made every customer feel favored.

Braam poured the wine.

"We never ever got our wine earlier," he said as they clinked glasses in a toast. "But I reckon we toasted each other anyway." He winked. "Cheers."

Debra almost chocked in the mouthful she had taken. Talk about innuendo.

"Ch-cheers," she said and swallowed her wine in a hurry. "Er, ooh, look here's our food."

"Saved by the tray?" Braam asked in a humorous tone.

"You bet."

"Then let's eat." Braam sat back whilst the waiter explained all the dishes then waved to Deb. "Help yourself, love. It will all be good."

She needed no more urging. He was right, it *was* good. More than good.

"Sheesh, I'm stuffed. How on earth will I be able to walk to the ferry?" Debra put her knife and fork down and sat back. "That was superb."

"Waddle with me. I always feel like that after eating here." Braam looked out of the plastic window. The rain was still falling like sheets of water. "Or paddle." He forked the last of his mutton curry and looked at the woman across the table. Her eyes were bright, her expression one of total satisfaction and she puffed her cheeks out and patted her tummy. He knew exactly what she meant. Moz's portions were never small and Braam was convinced the ones served to him were always bigger than most.

"Paddle, splash, I don't care. I think I love the rain." Debra winked. "Such interesting things happen in a rainstorm."

He couldn't argue with that. Braam grinned. "Do you want anything else? Moz's Balushahi are renowned all over..." He paused. "Lamma Island."

"Heh, I heard that, you slanderer you." Moz walked over to them and waggled his finger. "Lamma, Lantau *and* Hong Kong Island. I haven't quite cracked Kowloon yet, but I'm working on it. "So, you want Balushahi?"

Braam looked at Debra. "Do you?" He had to hold back his grin at her bewildered expression. "It's a sort of a doughnut. Hot and yummy."

Debra groaned. "That is cruel. I'm so full I could burst, but it sounds as if I have to try it."

"Shall we share one?" Braam suggested. "Take turns in biting?"

Deb blushed. He loved the way she did that.

"Yeah... However, don't expect me to move at any great speed for at least three days, mind. I won't want any more food for a fortnight at this rate."

Moz raised his hand in the air and signaled someone Braam couldn't see. Then he bent his head toward them both. "Sukhi calls them sex aids. Got to love my wife." He roared with laughter and bustled away.

"Sex aids?"

Braam rolled his eyes. "Sukhi has a warped sense of humor. For Moz's birthday one year, she made a set with holes in the middle of varying sizes and labeled them now, in a minute, ohhh let's go for it and all over now..."

Debra spluttered and put her wine glass down in a hurry. "Oh, well, maybe if we get some like that we could take them home for later."

Home? Oh, I like that idea.

Before Braam could answer, Moz came back with a steaming doughnut shaped cake on a plate and a brown paper bag.

"With love from Sukhi. She says you know what they mean." He winked. "All gluten free, of course." He waved away Braam's credit card. "No, my pleasure. You can return the favor when we get a night out together in Sai Kung."

"Gluten free?" Debra sounded puzzled.

"Yeah, well, I don't make a song and dance about it, but I'm coeliac. No wheat, rye or barley." Braam shrugged. "It's no biggie. I make sure I read labels."

"No pizza, baguettes or pasta?" Debra rolled her eyes as he shook his head. "Poor you."

"Hey, poor me, nothing. Better to find out why I had no energy, shitty low levels of iron and mouth ulcers after a visit to my favorite Italian restaurant. Now they do gluten free pasta and pizza in there and the supermarkets stock most things I need." Braam used the fork Moz had brought with the Balushahi to cut it in half. He broke a piece off, stabbed it with the fork and put it to Debra's mouth. Steam rose from the cake and even though she was full, the aroma was mouthwatering. "Here, inhale and enjoy. Mind, it's hot."

Debra closed her eyes as she took the mouthful. "Mmm-mmm." She muttered her appreciation around the sweet. "Grief, this is amazing. But I bet it's full of calories."

"Well not in that little bit." Braam took a bite himself and let the gorgeous spicy sweetness assail his taste buds. "But if it was all of it, well, who knows? That's why I need to help you out."

"Beast. You need to help me out so we can both walk as far as the ferry and not have to roll there." Debra picked another piece of Balushahi up and slid it slowly into her mouth. "Oh my, almost as great as s—" She stopped and grinned. "Sugar buns."

Her cheeky, sassy and sexual teasing was fun. Braam loved it. "Oh, honey, your buns aren't sugar, but they sure are great."

Debra stuck her tongue out at him. "I hope you mean great as in good and not as in size. Or I might be forced to do something drastic."

Braam wiped his finger through the sugary crumbs they'd left on the plate. Juvenile, but oh so satisfying. Why was it that those tiny morsels tasted so good and so illicit? He stood up and put the parcel of Balushahi into his backpack. "Sounds interesting. What exactly?"

Debra shouldered her own bag. "A-ha, that's for me to know and you to worry about."

He liked the sound of that.

* * * *

After waving their thanks to Moz who was still rushing round like a dervish, serving customers, they walked out of the restaurant, past the queue of people waiting for a table and along the quay that led to the ferry terminal. Already there was an untidy line of people around the gate.

"The next ferry is due in around ten minutes," Braam said as they walked past the stalls that lined the quay. A watery sun had appeared, even though dark clouds seemed to signal that it wouldn't be around for long. Even so, several stallholders had taken the opportunity to remove the makeshift plastic covers from their wares and were entreating anyone who went past to 'come in and look'.

Braam's emphatic shake of the head and his reply in Cantonese was as if an invisible signal passed down the row of stalls. After the first two or three, no one else bothered them.

"Hell, I'm sorry." He looked at Debra. "Did you want anything? I'm so used to saying no thank you, not today, I forgot you might want to look and shop. Slap me now."

Debra tapped his bum. "Naughty. Seriously, though, I'm fine. I made a vow at the beginning of my travels that it's one souvenir per place. It's certainly made me think before I part with my money."

Braam rubbed his arse with an exaggerated gesture and Debra rolled her eyes. "Aww, poor thing. Do you need me to kiss you better? You, not your arse."

How he loved the way they could act both silly and mature. Oh, and sexy. "You can kiss me and my arse any time you know. I'm agreeable."

She sniggered. "In your dreams."

"Oh, yeah." He twirled an imaginary mustache. "Oh, shit, here it comes. Can you run for it?" The sun disappeared behind one of the dark clouds that rolled over the horizon and joined those already nearby. "It's about to chuck it down."

"Sure."

Debra hitched her bag across her chest as Braam grabbed her hand and they ran like a pair of school kids toward the cover of the terminal. The surface was covered in puddles left behind from the last shower and they splashed through them, kicking up the water and laughing like a pair of idiots. By the time they reached cover and the rain came down in earnest, they were both soaked from their toes to their mid calves.

"We might have well walked and been wet all over," Debra said as they joined the end of the snaking queue.

"And probably not got on this ferry." Braam nudged her. "Look." Even in the short while since they'd taken their place, the queue had almost doubled. "Hold on here, I'll nip and get our tickets." He waved away her offer to buy them and walked briskly to the nearby ticket machine. Today was his treat. He stood not quite patiently whilst two Portuguese tourists tried to fathom out the instructions. At this rate, the ferry would have been and gone before he got their tickets. And the next one as well. He turned to the guy who was jabbing buttons like they were the enemy and spoke to him in his native language. The guy about fell on him with gratitude, as Braam showed him how to get tickets by buying his own and Debra's.

"What was that all about?" Debra asked him as he rejoined her. "That guy looked almost ready to give you his firstborn. Or offer his partner for sex. And he was about seven foot and eighteen stone."

"Yeah, I said thank you, but my wife wouldn't approve. Ah, they couldn't work out the instructions. Just in time."

The ferry approached the pier and the engines rumbled as it docked. The queue swayed like a bow wave as people jostled for position. Braam held on tightly to Debra's arm. It would be all too easy to become separated.

"Hold on, this could get uncomfortable." He lifted her off her feet and used his elbows for leverage.

It helped to know the local customs.

Chapter Seven

"I'm not sure how you managed that, but it was *very* well done," Debra said as they squashed onto a bench with a person who smelled of cheap cologne and an abundance of it at that.

The air was fuggy and redolent of damp people and wet dogs. The windows were steamy and streaked with rain. The waves were rolling and Debra hoped to hell she didn't get nauseated. On the way across she'd been too involved with Braam to even notice they were on water, but now it would be hard to miss the fact.

"Practice. The ferries from there are always busy, and with the rain I knew it'd be everyone for themselves. Even if there is in theory a queue, it soon disintegrates into a crowd. Oh, the boat will never be overloaded, not these days, but I'd rather us sit in reasonable comfort together, even if the atmosphere is a bit pungent. Anyway, we're almost there. No need to hurry. We'll take our time and let the crowd get off first. The ferry won't set off again with us still on it. They'd demand another fare before they did that."

Debra didn't doubt it. It was very popular. Braam had explained that the bigger village attracted more visitors than elsewhere on the island and therefore their ferries were always popular.

Several passengers stood, gathered bags and pushed each other in their eagerness to be first off. Why, Debra had no idea. The ferry wasn't even near the pier it docked at.

An oversized holdall, it couldn't be called a bag, swung perilously near her head. Debra ducked and Braam said something in what Debra had in mind might be Cantonese. Whatever language it was, it sounded annoyed. Cussing was cussing and she'd bet a pound that Braam had said something uncomplimentary.

"Arsehole. He needs a bag up his arse, because that's where his brain is. That poor kid on the other side of the aisle nearly got his ear removed. Yeah, I'd bugger off as well, you idiot. Before annoyed dad over there moves you with his boot." Braam shook his head. "Shit, ah, sorry, forgive my language, but sometimes. Anyway let him get off and out of the way. You never know, he might miss the gangplank, slip over the side and get some sense washed into him."

Debra glanced out of the window. "I don't think he'll need to slip over the side. It's raining like stair rods out there." Maybe she'd better get her rain jacket out. It was as well that earlier she'd owned up to having one. Then it was fun to ignore it and she wouldn't have missed the outcome for anything, but now she didn't relish a soaking.

The ferry commenced its forwards and backwards shuffles as it lined up to the dock and soon the crowd thinned.

"Got your coat handy?" Braam asked her. "We'll never get a taxi around here and to be honest, I love walking in the rain." He gave her a look, which Debra could only describe as enigmatic.

She tugged her cost out of her bag. "Yep. You?"

"I will have before we get out of the terminal. Okay, let's make a move before they do demand another fare from us." He stood up and propelled Debra forward with a hand on her butt. That gesture might be innocent, but the suggestive squeeze that followed wasn't. How on earth she didn't wriggle back into Braam's touch, Debra had no idea. She must have made some sort of noise because he bent his head to whisper into her ear.

"Later. Hold that thought."

"Oh, I intend to," Debra said as she stepped off the ferry and onto the gangplank that went up and down with the swell of the waves. "Where shall I hold it, though?" She looked over her shoulder at Braam and staggered as one wave bigger than the others suddenly lifted the gangplank and threw it back down again.

"Woops." She spread her legs a little farther, regained her balance, took hold of the rope that ran up one side of the swaying planking and hurried onto dry land.

"Careful or it'll be you getting a ducking, not arsehole." Braam joined her and they made their way up the steep slope to street level. Behind them the ferry was already filling up rapidly with its new passengers.

"Give me a minute to get my coat on and we'll brave the elements." Braam took a black waterproof out of his bag and put it on. Then he turned to Debra and pulled her hood over her hair. "There. Shall we?"

"Okay." She shook her head until the hood slipped back and landed on her neck. "I hate my head covered. It's rain, not hailstones or anything nasty. Now, if it were my arms it would be a different matter. Which way?"

"Across there. If we walk toward town we might hit lucky and grab a taxi. Otherwise it's squeeze onto a tram or an MTR."

"Or walk." They linked arms and set off. Once they were away from the water, the wind died down and the rain didn't seem as heavy.

"It's a long way," Braam said with a note of warning in his voice. "And we've done a fair bit already."

"True." She sniggered. "And we've walked four k as well. But I will if you will."

"Oh, always."

She punched his arm. "Idiot. I mean I'm okay to walk."

"What else," Braam said gravely. His eyes were full of devilment. "Well, let's see how we go. At least I know some shortcuts."

Not only did he know some shortcuts, he knew some deserted alleys where a kiss and a very satisfactory grope, all above board, or as Debra thought to herself above clothes helped them on their way.

The rain stopped and the humidity—and her libido—rose. It wasn't long before Debra was sweating, although whether that was owing to the humidity or Braam's words and actions she couldn't decide. A bit of both probably.

Braam stopped to take her jacket from her and stow it with his in his bag. He put his finger over her lips. "No arguing please. We've not got long to go now. Look." He hesitated. "As much as I'd like to spend the evening with you, I have appointments I can't get out of and tomorrow is going to be hellish busy. Will you meet me in the gym in the morning?"

Is this the start of the end? The beginning of 'it was nice to know you, in every sense of the word and don't let the doorknob hit you in the arse on your way out'?

"I can see the cogs whirring," Braam said as they turned into the street where the hotel was situated. "I pushed and shoved to get today off. Yes, I was due several days, but various developments mean I'll have to postpone them. And as I'd like a couple of days—and nights—with you sooner, rather than later, if I get this crisis sorted, we're more likely to get them. Bear with me, love, please?" He kissed her nose and stroked her cheek.

Now if you nuzzle my neck, I'm a goner.

He nuzzled her neck.

Argh.

Debra moaned and gasped. Braam laughed. "You're a mix of shows and tells, love, and I'm beginning to understand them. I'm not looking for a get out clause, I *am* pissed off at having to work, but it is my job. I'll come and kiss you goodnight."

"Now that's an offer I can't refuse. Will you tuck me in as well?"

"I might even tell you a goodnight story. Right, are you walking in with me or doing your cloak and dagger skulking?"

"Skulking? Ha, skulking indeed," Debra said, very tongue in cheek. "There I am, trying to protect your reputation as, as a, whatever it needs protecting as and you say I'm skulking. Which is an archaic word anyway." She poked him in the chest. "And no, you can take yourself back. I'm sure you'll manage. I'm going in here." She pointed to a tiny mini market.

For the first time since she'd started to tease him, a frown appeared on his face.

Oh shit, he thinks I'm serious and annoyed. It was her turn to kiss his nose, even though she had to hold onto his shoulders for balance and stretch up on her toes. "The reason I'm going in here is because I have no lemon for gin and tonic and I want to get something snacky and gluten free. The hotel I'm staying in charges an arm and a leg for a gin out of the mini bar and they don't even think of lemon. My lover deserves the best, even if he is simply popping in to give me a goodnight kiss."

He snickered, but his relief was evident. "And tuck you in and tell you a bedtime story."

"And that. Seriously, though, I don't want to do anything to ruin your reputation."

"Honey, you couldn't, but I understand. I feel that about you. Okay, then I'll hopefully see you later. If I can't make it, I'll ring you."

"Let me give you my mobile number." Debra rattled it off and he blinked.

"Give me a sec. I don't have a great memory for instant numbers." He took out his phone and as she repeated them, tapped it in. "Great. Right I'll leave you to your lemon buying. By the way, I like salted popcorn and plain crisps." He kissed her again and walked down the street, a tall, blond, good-looking man, who had more than one woman staring as he passed.

Debra walked into the shop deep in thought. That would always be the effect he had on people. Why then had he singled her out? He could get anyone he fancied, surely, even if he didn't want to get serious. She picked up a lemon and some popcorn and checked the packs of crisps for gluten as she gave herself a strict talking to. She had to get over the why me and think wow me, instead.

What else should she buy? Debra accepted that even though she wasn't hungry, she needed to eat out of her room. Therefore she'd go to the restaurant and have a salad or something light. There was no way she would go until the morning without her tummy rumbling. The thought that she might get a glimpse of Braam didn't influence her choice. Well, not too much.

Another shop across the street caught her eye and she smiled. Oh yes. She'd been meaning to go in there for ages. Perhaps—no amend that, definitely—time to open her purse. She'd buy two souvenirs from Hong Kong, not one.

* * * *

As she sat on a soft settee after her meal and listened to the pianist playing, Debra kept one eye on her eReader and the other on the lookout for Braam. Her meal had been superb—she thought. Now, an hour after she ate, she wasn't sure what had been on her plate. Rosemary potatoes and something chickeny? Probably. She'd given the salad a miss but did have a glass of a dry Sancerre and declined a sweet.

Now she sat with a coffee, because she thought another glass of wine and she'd fall asleep. The day of fresh air and fantastic sex had tired her out. Debra masked another yawn and finished the coffee. If she didn't leave the lounge, she'd fall asleep where she was. That would cause a stir.

Every bone in her body ached and she winced as she stood up. All the unaccustomed exertion of every type was now reminding her why she said exercise was a dirty word. She either had to do more or do none.

Maybe it best be more. After all, it was never too late to get fit, especially if it involved a younger, sexy, hot bod man who could tell you what to do and how. As well as appreciating your input.

Debra passed her thanks to the barman and wandered, as slowly as she could and not be thought to be loitering, toward the lift. Opposite the lift doors was the reception.

As ever, two smartly dressed receptionists sat there. One looked up as Debra waited for the lift to arrive and smiled.

"Had a good day, Mrs. Scotburn?"

"Oh, yes, thank you. Lots of fresh air and exercise. It's an early night, I think."

The lift arrived and the doors opened. Debra stepped inside and slid her key card into the slot to activate the lift.

"Hold it, please. Ah, Mrs. Scotburn, how are you? Have you had a good day?" Braam got into the lift next to her and winked. He was still dressed in the shirt and shorts he wore earlier and there were weary lines in his face. "What floor do you want?"

"Oh, er, the terrace please. I need some fresh air after my dinner."

He knew what she meant. Not that he'd managed any dinner. The moment he'd stepped inside the hotel, the new manager had asked for his help. He hadn't even managed to pull on a pair of trousers and it felt wrong to be inside the hotel, sort of on duty and dressed so casually. It had been well over an hour before he had the chance to even open his own emails and a further hour to work through them and now he had to answer the most important. He still had at least another hour's work before he could happily call it a night.

"I wish I could join you," he spoke softly. "And I also wish to hell that this bloody lift didn't have security cameras in it. But it does."

Debra swayed. "Oh fu — er, damn, perhaps as well I didn't follow my first inclination then."

He raided one eyebrow in inquiry. "Which was?"

She bent down to fiddle with her shoe. As she stood up she held onto the wall so her mouth was close to him. "To jump you." She raised her voice. "Are you going to the terrace, Mr. Van Meister? I hear it's a great place to walk in the evening."

"Alas no, I'm going for a well needed shower and then back to work for an hour before I can relax."

The lift stopped and he stood back to let Debra precede him out onto the terrace foyer.

"All work and all that," she said.

He nodded. "Oh, yes, which is why I'm going to get the work done as soon as possible." He gave a half bow, drank in her smile and watched her stroll toward the terrace walking track before he turned toward his suite.

He really did need that shower.

The trouble was he kept imagining what it would be like to share it with Debra. To take the bar of soap and run it over her body and soap up the sponge and circle her breasts and rub between her legs. To sit her on the ledge and kiss her senseless. Then turn her around and rub his cock over the luscious globes of her ass, before slipping between them and...

The soap slid from his hands and onto the floor of the shower with a thump. Braam jerked and his cock hit the wall of the shower. The pain was totally unexpected and surely too excessive for what had happened. But then it was as hard as timber and ready for action. Maybe not that sort of action.

Braam swore and turned off the water. *Bugger it, she'll be the death of me.*

He stepped out of the cubicle and wrapped a towel around his waist. If she was going to be the death of him, he was going to make sure it was a pleasurable death. And happen sooner rather than later. But first he had to finish work. At least he didn't have to go downstairs to do that.

He dragged on a clean shirt and jeans, set up his laptop and tried to involve himself in work, but he couldn't settle. The thought of Debra on the terrace by herself didn't sit comfortably with him. Even though once he realized she often went there late in the evening he'd arranged for a security guard to be on duty.

He made his mind up and dialed her room number.

He was about to hang up when Debra answered. She sounded breathless.

"'Lo?"

"Hi."

She giggled somewhat choppily. "Am I supposed to add silver lining? Oh, no, that's the other way round, or nearly anyway. Er, who is this? Are you a heavy breathing phone call?"

Sometimes she was so damned difficult to follow. Braam ignored the first part of her reply and homed in on the second.

"Would you like me to be?"

"We—ell. Only if you follow it up."

He laughed. "I wish. It's going to be about another hour I guess before I can finish for the day and not feel guilty I've missed something. Will you still be awake?"

"Ah. Let's see, hi...ho...and silver lining. Is there one? Well now, there's one way to find out now, isn't there." The line went dead.

Braam shook his head. How could any man understand the workings of a female mind? Hi, ho, silver lining? He got the connection and was sure he had a stupid, sappy look on his face as he went back to work.

This time he blocked everything out except work. It wasn't going to be long before he was moved to wherever the next crisis was looming. He wasn't the computer guru and he'd done almost as much as he could to find out what had been happening at the hotel. Lax security, not enough supervision and a massive case of lust for the head receptionist seemed to have tipped the ex-manager over the edge into crime. Braam had mostly fixed the first two and shuddered at the thought of the third. The new manager had a lot more rules and regulations to follow. Channing Hotels always learned from past mistakes. Even though there hadn't been many, there would be a lot fewer in the future.

Braam stretched his arms above his head, checked his watch and groaned. He'd been so involved in tying up as many ends as he could, he hadn't been aware how much time had passed. He'd be lucky if Debra would let him through the door. If she was awake. It was after midnight. Still, he was going to see. At least he'd showered and changed earlier, so it was a matter of minutes to leave his room and go down a few levels to hers.

He rang the buzzer and leaned on the wall as he waited to see if she would answer the door. Half of him hoped he hadn't woken her up. The other half hoped if she was asleep, he had.

Contrary bastard.

The door swung open and his tiredness dropped off him. "What the hell would you have done if it wasn't me?" he asked hoarsely. The sheer black item of clothing she wore barely covered the bits of her that needed covering in public.

"Asked if you had a twin. I looked through the peephole." Debra stood back to let Braam into the room. She looked at his face as she closed the door and curtseyed. "What's up, Braam. Don't you like it?"

"I think 'like' is a bit lukewarm, love. I'm not entirely sure what it is, but I love it."

Debra walked around him and did a twirl. The hem of the garment flicked up and showed tantalizing glimpses of her bum and pussy. She stopped abruptly and leaned on him.

"Whew, twirling after a glass of wine is maybe not the best thing to do. I get giddy enough being near you without adding to it." She raised her eyebrows and licked her lips. "If you get my meaning."

"Every time, love." Braam held her arms and pulled her close for a hug. "Likewise with me. I feel eighteen and scared and about to discover how a man and a woman mesh. Twenty-five and wondering what next and thirty-two and thinking, why me? All mixed in together and damned humbling as I ask how the hell I could be so bloody lucky."

"Aw." Debra sniffed, as his sincere words hit her. "It's strange isn't it, how you can think you're perfectly happy as things are. Then you meet someone and know that all along you were waiting for that person. Then it's scary, scary, because you don't want to screw things up. Added to the worries of does he like me, like I like him. Will he laugh at me for liking furry toys and having to use kids' chopsticks? Can he cope with me singing out of tune and always scoffing the red jelly babies first? Does he mind me being so much older? All important stuff like that."

"Well, most of it's fine. But the red jelly babies?" Braam shook his head and put his finger on his cheek. "That's definitely a negotiable subject. Do you save the orange ones till last?"

"The orange ones?" Debra did her best to sound shocked. "I don't like those. Nah, the best ones are blackcurrant and I hoard them. Er, would I need to share?"

Braam sat down on her settee and lifted her onto his lap. "Well now, what's it worth?"

He kissed the nape of her neck. Debra determined there and then that it was her new erogenous zone. The soft touch, the warm breath that stirred her hair, the shivers and tingles he gave her, all combined to make her body stir and want more. She twisted around on his lap and he groaned as his cock hardened beneath her ass. Debra loved the sexy sound. She wriggled a bit more.

"Enough, woman. This is supposed to be me tucking you in and giving you a cuddle not fu—making love." Braam held her firmly against him. "If you continue wriggling, I'm not going to be accountable for my actions."

Debra tried to wriggle again, but Braam held her tight.

"No more, Deb, please. I've still got to do a last check around before I turn in."

It was the look on his face that made her sit still. She wasn't being fair.

"Sorry. Take my word for it, I'm happy you got here anyway. I was going to say I'm glad you came, but maybe that's not the right word?"

He chuckled. "Well, I did earlier. More than once. Now, though, I need to go." He stood up, still holding her and dropped her gently on the bed. Debra bounced.

"Damn, there I was hoping my souvenir of Hong Kong was going to be so irresistible you'd succumb to my wiles and charms and stay."

Braam ran his hands through his hair. She'd observed that particular action when he was worried or thinking hard.

"Braam, it's okay. I know you're busy. This," she ran her hand over her teddy, "was as much for me as you. I thought it was time I ditched the granny jammies. I've been lusting over this in that wee shop in the arcade ever since I arrived. I've been careful how I spent my money and made up my mind it was me time. Well, me for you time."

"Will you join me in the gym tomorrow?"

The chance of subject surprised her. She'd seen the wicked glint in his eyes and the way he'd adjusted his cock under his jeans. He hadn't tried to hide his actions.

"In this?" Debra asked. "That would maybe cause a bit of talk."

"As tempting as it is, maybe not. Although I want to meet there before it opens to the general public. Will you?" He knelt on the bed next to her. "And save this for another night? I'm going to have wet dreams and fantasies about how I'm going to take you whilst you wear it, take you as I strip you out of it." He stroked her over the silk around her nipples and down toward her pussy. "And make love to you as you lie naked on top of it."

He stood up and walked to the door. "Have I now got a fetish about you and black silk? You bet." He blew her a kiss. "Six a.m. The gym. Don't be late."

Debra threw a pillow in the general direction of the door as it shut behind him.

How the hell was she supposed to be able to get to sleep after all that? Apart from anything else, what did you wear to the gym when you didn't exercise?

* * * *

It seemed Braam had an idea. His text woke her a few minutes before her alarm.

That little flirty skirt I saw you in the other day and a vest top would be ideal for our gym appointment. How do you get on with the exercise machines?

That was easy.

We've never been introduced and I was always told I needed to be introduced first.

Ha ha. Get your cute little self up here.

She could imagine him saying the words as he typed and just about saw the glint in his eyes in her mind.

She took out the skirt he'd mentioned and looked at it in doubt. It was shortish and the hem was barely above her knees. Perfectly respectable, with underwear and a bra. But with nothing except a vest top? She'd wobble and jiggle all over the place and even the slightest breeze might cause embarrassment.

Should she or shouldn't she? Debra pulled it on and added a vest top. As she thought, her boobs needed the support of a bra. She was no stick insect, far from it. A twist and a shake in front of the mirror confirmed her thoughts. A bra was a must. She could probably get away without any knickers as long as she walked slowly and decorously and made sure she kept her legs close together. But did he mean that? Was she reading sexual innuendo and banter where there wasn't any intended?

The pinging of her phone to indicate a text made her jump. In her introspective mood, Debra decided her boobs jerked so high they nearly took her eye out.

Oh, enough already. She opened the message.

Ah, love, I'm sorry to tease you. Come as you feel comfortable. I need to exercise and I thought even if it's not your thing, you could be here with me to encourage me. Otherwise I'd be skiving off to share your bed and who knows when we'd get out! See you when you get here.

She could understand what he meant. They did have a habit of getting carried away, and she rather liked it. It was so not the old Debra and so part of how she now felt. Braam had dragged her out of her comfort zone, shot her complacent 'I don't do anything non-conforming' attitude to smithereens and woke up a part of her she'd thought long gone. Debra took a deep breath, slid her feet into trainers—at least they'd look the part—grabbed her room fob and left before she could change her mind.

Chapter Eight

Would she come? If so what would she wear? Should he have sent that text? Was it too suggestive, cheeky, presumptuous, tacky or out of order? How did he know, really know if she could see the humor and the need in those few words? Loving someone so soon after meeting them, and pushing both of you way out of your comfort zone was hard and bloody scary. Braam switched the lights on in the gym, checked the blinds were down, made sure the notice about opening hours was clearly displayed outside and proceeded to go through his warm up as he waited to see if Debra turned up.

By the time he'd spent fifteen minutes increasing his speed on the treadmill, Braam was beginning to get worried and annoyed. The noise of the air conditioning unit as it cut in and out irritated him. It showed the passing of time.

Where was she? Had she made her mind up he was too everything she didn't like? Then he looked at the clock. It was still early and a good ten minutes before the time they had agreed on. That fact didn't seem to help his mood. He poured a paper cone full of water, drank it, then dragged a couple of exercise mats and blanket into a heap next to the rowing machine. If she turned up at least it would be semi-comfortable to sit on.

If she turns up? Where is she?

He poured another cone full of water and thought of Debra. There was so much he wanted to learn about her and there was so little time. She would be leaving to go back to Scotland soon and goodness knows when he'd have time to go there to meet up with her again. Would it be fair to ask her to travel to wherever he happened to be, knowing they'd have to snatch time together? It was a dilemma he wasn't sure they could solve.

Where the hell is she? Does she have to leave it to the last minute? Does she not want to be here with me? Why am I so pissy?

He knew why. Because it mattered.

The bell outside the gym door rang loudly. Braam swore as he was jerked out of his reverie and once more cold water dripped down his chest and onto his cock. Talk about déjà vu.

He stalked stiff-legged to the door and opened it wide. He was mad and could think of no reason why. If it was Debra, she was here. She'd turned up so why the chip on his shoulder? He had no idea.

Debra stared at him in wide-eyed disbelief.

He could imagine what he looked like. Sweaty and soaked, but luckily not sporting a hard-on. Not yet.

"I didn't think you showered until you finished exercising. And even then you stripped out of your gym kit. Have I missed something?" Debra sauntered passed him and spun around to look him in the face.

Braam shut the door by the simple method of kicking it. It banged solidly and rattled the frame.

"Missed something? Now why would you think that?" He knew his voice was furious. Damn it, he *was* furious and he had no bloody idea why. She was dressed as he'd asked and looked hot. Her boobs were unfettered and enticed him to touch and feast. In all his wildest fantasies he hadn't dared imagine that.

Get a grip.

"I have no idea," Debra said in an even tone.

It made him want to throw something, anything, or rant and rave like a tantrum filled teen. And for why? *Too much too soon? Scared and pathetic?*

"However, you look as if you can't decide whether to screw me or show me the door. I'll tell you what, let me decide for you, eh?"

He did? She was what?

"Who do you think you're talking to? I'm not one of your kids you can order around."

"No, my kids behave much more maturely, and I wouldn't dream of ordering them to do anything. Sheesh." She shook her head and the long dangly earrings he'd admired jangled. "Argh, fuck off, Braam. I don't know what's got stuck up your arse, but it's got B—all to do with me." She walked, very upright and with a determined step past him, then wrenched at the door. Her face was whiter than the pile of clean towels on the cupboard top and her red lips stood out, to accuse him of every awful thing imaginable.

Unfortunately for her, and damned lucky for him, he'd set the door to lock automatically.

"Open the fucking door, Braam." Debra tugged and turned the handle, anger in every jerky movement she made.

"No. And you think that's suitable language?" Why was he adding fuel to the fire? Did he have a death wish? No, he needed her to shoot him down, pick him up and be his.

"Oh, yes."

Braam bit his angry retort back. She didn't deserve it.

She spun back and that floaty skirt flicked way too high for his libido to cope with.

"Speak to the hand, buddy." She gave him two fingers. "It's all you're fit for. What on earth is eating you? You asked me to turn up. I got out of my bed at silly o'clock and for what? A bucket of grief. What is *eating* you? And open the sodding door." She kicked it with her trainer-covered foot and winced. "Sheesh, what's it made of, concrete?"

The look she gave him would have felled a lesser man. The sheen of tears in her eyes felled him.

"Oh, God, Deb, I'm so sorry," he said hoarsely. He walked across to her and tried to take her in his arms.

She brushed them away as if she was flicking a speck of dust and stared, stony-faced, at him.

"Go away. I have a mad. A big, hot in my gut, want to thump you mad." She sniffed and dug in her pocket, to bring out a tissue and blow her nose. "Bastard."

"You're right, I am. You've done nothing wrong and everything right." How on earth could he explain it, when he didn't know himself what he was trying to explain? "It's me and I've no idea why I'm like this. Well, except I'm scared you don't feel the same way, worried how we're going to sort the future out, concerned I'll be sent to darkest wherever is farthest from you and I'm as horny as a rhino. Only for you, Deb, only for you. Please don't go." He finished in a flat monotone. "Hell, don't cry. I'm not worth it." Braam wiped his thumb across the tears under her eyes. It cut him so deeply to see her like this and know it was all down to him.

She bit her lip. "You, Mr. Van M, are an idiot. You so are. Worth it. We are." She took hold of his hand and he folded his fingers around it. It was warm and soft and to his sorrow it shook. "But hello? This is hard. You make it almost impossible to, well, to get to know you. There's a great big wall to climb and I'm scared of heights without a safety net." She bit her lip and refused to look him in the eyes.

"Shit, Deb, am I such an ogre?" Braam was appalled at what he had done. "I scare you and make you shake?"

She stared him in the face. He couldn't decipher her expression.

"Tell me," he said as he looked at her and wished he could kick himself for causing the misery he could see in her eyes. "Please, for God's sake, tell me."

She sighed. "No, no ogre. Merely a complicated man who doesn't wear his heart on his sleeve. Break down the wall, Braam. Then tell me, what exactly do you want?"

"You," he said instantly. "You, with me."

She looked doubtful. How the hell could he reassure her?

"I know there's no reason for you to believe me. If I knew why I was such an idiot, I'd tell you. I don't have a dodgy past. I have no reason to block you out of my life. Well, except for some work-related stuff. But why should you trust my word? Especially after I've acted like I have today. For no good reason. Well, except that you matter."

"Well you've got a crappy way of showing it."

Debra stared at him for so long, Braam wanted to fidget. Finally she walked past him to the water cooler, filled a paper cone and turned back to him.

"I should throw this over you and walk away. After all, life is too short to back a loser. But you know?" she sighed. "I can't."

Braam let out the breath he hadn't been aware he held and moved toward her. Debra held up her hand.

"Hold on. I expect more of a grovel." She looked at him speculatively.

He grinned warily and was pleased when she half smiled back. Her face had lost its pinched look and the color that had leeched out when he'd torn into her was coming back.

"Mea culpa? I owe you chocolate?"

"That's a mini grovel. I want a great big one."

Braam got down on his knees in front of her. The floor was hard and he wondered whether he'd need help getting up. That would be enough to spoil any grand gesture. "I, Abraham Van Meister, do humbly grovel at the feet of Debra Scotburn. To apologize for my pissy, up myself mood and admit there was no reason for it except my own self-doubt. Not doubt about how I feel about her, which is very deeply, but myself. As in why me?"

"Hmm." Debra knelt down next to him. "It's a start. However, you still owe me chocolate. And something else."

He hoped to hell she didn't want to see him bleed. Because he knew his reputation would be shot to bits if she did. He went giddy at the sight of blood.

"Champagne? Dinner at Sun Tung Lok?" He named a nearby Michelin starred restaurant. "My head on a plate?"

"Maybe, oh wow and no, not your head or a plate." Debra pinched his ear. "What I want…" She paused and tilted her head to one side. "Is…"

Braam held his breath.

"You."

He swallowed. His mouth was dry and his skin clammy. "Me? As in…?" His words came out in a croak. Braam cleared his throat and began again. "I mean, how?"

"Like this."

He could hardly believe his eyes. Debra looked around the gym and made a noise deep in her throat. He could only liken it to a purr.

"Over there, I think." She pointed to the exercise mats and blanket he'd heaped together earlier. "I won't make you crawl, although in the last book I read it sounded fun."

Crawl?

"Oh, love, you've had me crawling this last half hour or so, believe me."

"Then enough is enough." Debra stood up and held her hand out to him. "I guess we can say we've had our first row?"

He nodded and wondered what she was thinking. The look on her face was serene and gave no indication of what was in her mind.

"Good then, now we need makeup sex."

We do? Oh yes we do.

"As in here and now makeup sex? I'm forgiven?"

"Well, once we have makeup sex you will be. So?"

"Love, you humble me."

"No, no humbling, I want a big, strong man to take me to heaven again. And I'm sure you're the man to do that. I've even brought something with me to help you." Debra put her hand inside a pocket of her skirt he hadn't noticed and brought out a foil packet. "In case you needed one."

"Snap." He slipped his fingers into the pocket sewn into the waistband of his running shorts. It was supposed to be for an MP3 player but it was very versatile. "In case my fantasy came true."

Debra ran her fingers over the handle of the exercise bike. The tactile way she did it, made Braam wish he were the recipient not the bike. She looked at him from under her lowered lashes.

"And has it?"

"Not quite yet, but I live in hope. Your skirt plays a big part. So does the purple peril over there." He nodded toward the colorful Pilates ball in the corner. His heart and his cock swelled as her eyes widened and she gave a slow and incredibly wicked grin.

"The Pilates ball? How?" She didn't sound mad, but definitely interested.

"May I show you?" Braam stroked her cheek. The tiny touch was something he couldn't have enough of. Her soft skin almost vibrated as he skimmed across the surface. She leaned into the curve of his palm and sighed a needy moan.

"Oh yeah."

Funny how once you made your mind up to forgive, forget and act like an adult, things all slipped into place. Well, Debra amended in her mind, so far they had. There was one, much more important thing that needed to slip into place. His cock into her pussy. How that was going to happen and involve the Pilates ball, she had no idea. But was desperate to find out.

Oh, God, I'm acting like a sex-starved man-hungry predator. And I love it. Well not the predator bit and not the starved bit but, ohh, shut up. Debra squashed her thoughts and let herself concentrate on Braam, his touch and the here and now.

A sudden thought made her slow down at the same time as Braam set off to take her toward the ball.

"The door?"

"Still locked," Braam reassured her.

"People wanting to get in?"

"We don't open today until eight. It's one of the deep clean days."

"Deep clean?"

He flicked her nose. "Where we do more than the everyday cleaning. Every other day, it's almost like a shut up shop and repaint job. Without the paint. Enigma did it last night when it closed because he wants to go to his sister's husband's cousin's son's wedding celebrations early today. I said fine and I'd check it was all okay this morning for him."

As much as she wanted to know the difference between a thorough clean and a deep clean and who Enigma was, Debra reckoned it could wait. She wanted to know the difference between making love and involving a Pilates ball and making love and not.

"Um, so you thought of everything? Ah, good. Oh yeah."

"Well, I'm hoping you'll agree it's very good. I thought of so many things. How you'd look naked and on top of the massage table. Whether the vibrating plates over there would help or hinder us." Braam had slipped his hand under her skirt. "How your skin would color and whether you get red all over and... Damn, Deb, it's as well I wasn't totally sure you were buck naked or I'd have had you over the seat of the weight bench ages ago." He started to knead and stroke each globe of her ass, hard enough to send a shiver and a surge of red-hot arousal through her.

The weight bench? "Ah, right, well I'm glad you didn't. I'm much more interested in the Pilates ball. I'm sort of fond of purple."

"I'll be even fonder soon." He rolled the ball around with the hand not playing with her rear. "How supple are you? Don't look as if I've asked you if you can run down the central escalator whilst it's going up."

Debra closed her mouth that she'd let drop open at his question. Her? Supple? Actually, even though she wasn't an exercise freak, she was reasonably fit. She enjoyed walking and although she didn't do a lot of bending and lifting, what she did do, she did well. After all her protestations that exercise was a dirty word, she might be about to surprise him.

"Hmm, let me see. What about this?" She measured the distance in her mind and with a wink, lay face down over the ball with her ass in the air. She made sure her skirt barely covered her rear.

It was weird with her boobs squished against the PVC, her face dangling over the other side of the ball and her toes on the floor to give her any balance. Debra let her feet rise and fall so the ball moved forward and back a little.

The air conditioning cut out in its cycle. The silence was almost absolute. Except for the soft squeak of PVC on floor tiles, Braam's sharp intake of breath and his reverent, "Oh my, yeah."

She wriggled her butt and giggled. Oh, was she enjoying teasing him.

"But if I'm like this, how will you play with me?" She knew *she* was playing with fire. "Oh, that's no good. I know." She swung around until her back was on the ball and her legs were at ninety degrees from it, with her feet on the floor. She wriggled until she was sure she had her balance and used her hands to anchor the ball in place.

"I don't know if this is enough suppleness?" She deliberately lowered her voice and was pleased with the result. Whoever would have guessed that listening to an old program about an ex UK prime minister and how she'd reinvented herself would bring off such a result?

"More than. Can you keep yourself like this?" Braam lifted the hem of her skirt and rubbed her clit. Debra mewled as her juices gathered and she pushed into his touch.

"Don't fall off now." He grinned, put his hands on the floor either side of her and bent his head. His tongue swirled around her clit then the tip entered her vagina far enough for her to arch her back and gasp. The feeling of his tongue pushing into her, the way his teeth grazed her skin and the gentle rocking of the ball, sent skitters of red-hot arousal through her. Her body was on fire, her climax building faster than a tidal wave hit the shore. She couldn't thrash her head around as she wanted to. She panted and muttered incoherently as Braam continued his relentless pressure on her pussy.

The noise of foil tearing barely registered in her mind. The way he moved away from her did. She felt cold and lost and she must have made some noise of disapproval because Braam spoke near her ear.

"Give me a second, love. I haven't left you, you're not cold and I'm going to warm us both up even more. Hold on now, let's go for a ride."

All of a sudden her legs were lifted off the floor. Debra steadied herself with her hands and thanked every god in the world that they'd backed the ball to the wall. Although she might roll off sideways, she'd not fall front wise onto her ass. She had to hope she didn't bang her head.

"Oh so ready for me." Braam crooned the words. "My cock is oh so ready to fill you. Look, feel." The tip of his cock teased the entrance to her channel and the length of it slid into her as if it was coming home.

In a way, Debra thought hazily, it was.

Then Braam moved. He set up a steady thrust where each push sent him a little farther into her. Debra matched him as she clenched and relaxed her muscles to help him and her.

The rock of the ball, the thrusting of Braam, his harsh breathing and the sensations that bombarded her sent Debra into a vortex she hadn't known existed. Her body shuddered as her climax overtook her. Colored lights flashed under her eyelids and she dimly heard a voice screaming, "Yes... Mine..."

Then Braam shuddered and gave one long, hard thrust. Deb tightened her legs around him and held him deep inside her.

"Ah... Yes, mine."

Oh and mine.

How long they stayed like that, Debra wasn't certain. Neither did she care. The facts that her bottom half was naked, that Braam was still buried inside her and that some time soon the gym would maybe have people hammering on the door and demanding to be let in didn't bother her one bit.

The air con switched on and cold air hit her butt. She shivered. She hadn't registered whether it was on or off whilst she and Braam made love, but now? Now she wanted to throw something at the switch.

Braam stirred. "Hold on, we need to move. Or I do, or I'll get all over excited again and I don't think these condoms are two timers. Although in the coming in you sense, not the cheating on you sense, I reckon I could be."

So did she. His cock hadn't softened that much and Debra was of a mind that with a few judicious muscle clenches and wriggles they could go another round. However, the mention of condoms was a blast of cold reason.

She held her tongue and herself still, as Braam pulled out and swore. "Shit we need to move. Hell and damnation, love, I hadn't realized how long I could last for." He didn't sound that perturbed. "I need to have that door open in twenty minutes max. Let me get rid of the condom and then help you up."

It was nice of him to think of her, but Debra thought she'd better try to help herself a bit. She didn't bother to open her eyes as she let her arms go loose and slid onto the floor. It was chilly and she shivered. Hot sex was fantastic — cold floors and air, not so much.

"Hey, I said I'd help. Come on, oops a daisy."

Her world behind her eyelids tilted. Her nostrils filled with the earthy, all male scent of Braam. She inhaled deeply. *Perfect.* Debra opened one eye a millimeter and watched the walls of the gym move past her. She smiled to herself. That was a stupid thing to think.

"As much as I'd love to shower with you, I don't think we've got time." Braam set her onto her feet.

Debra swayed.

"Here, hold onto me." Braam held her steady until she believed the walls weren't moving and her legs would hold her.

"Okay now." Debra wasn't positive her voice was strong enough to confirm the truth behind her words.

"Sure?" It seemed Braam wasn't certain either.

She nodded. "If I can wash my face and tidy myself, I think I'll head back to my suite to shower. After all, nobody would believe I've done any exercise, *on the machines,*" she emphasized the words as Braam raised one eyebrow. "Dressed like this," she finished.

"You have a point." He'd put on some loose sweat pants over his shorts and a T-shirt over the vest he'd worn. Whatever state his cock was now in, the sweats hid it well.

He looked hot in all the best ways. Debra gave into impulse and wound her hands around his neck. "You make me feel young and sexy. May I say how good that is?"

"And back, love, and back. Though I'm glad I know what I know now and don't have to rely on what I knew then."

She could relate to that.

"Right, let's get this door unlocked so if anyone does turn up on the dot, we'll look all above board." He did as he'd said, then turned to Debra with a wicked glint in his eye.

"So, Mrs. Scotburn, what do you think of the facilities and the equipment? Oh hello, Mr. Brinkman, how are you this morning?"

Debra swung round to face a closed door and nobody about.

"You sod." She punched his shoulder and giggled. "I died a hundred deaths then. I suddenly realized that my skirt was ruched up and my arse was probably on show." She tugged the offending garment down. "As for the equipment? Oh, in perfect condition. The facilities? Very interesting."

The door opened and a tall middle-aged man entered the room and let the door swing closed behind him. Debra gulped and stifled a grin. "Thank you so much for showing me around, Mr. Van Meister. I'll certainly think about using the gym." She held out her hand as the newcomer walked past them and climbed on the cross trainer. Braam took her hand and scribed erotic circles over the back of it. Debra scowled as he grinned. That wasn't going to help her get out of the room without stumbling.

"That's good. As you can see there's something for everyone." His left eyelid closed so briefly that she wasn't sure he had winked.

Debra bit her lip to hold back the laugh she so wanted to give.

Braam lowered his voice. "I'll text you later." He opened the door and held it ajar.

"That's fine, I'll remember."

It was hard to walk sedately to the lift. Only the fact that she was mindful of the chance of other people appearing kept her feet firmly on the ground and her back straight. Skipping and showing her bits wouldn't be a good idea.

Before she had a chance to press the button to call the lift, the doors opened and several people got out. One or two of them looked at her in astonishment. Well, okay, she wasn't dressed appropriately for the gym — well not in the conventional way — but who was to say she hadn't been using the laundry?

Debra got into the lift and pressed her floor button before anyone said anything. Her tummy rumbled and she pressed her hand over it. She was starving. There was something about an early morning workout that had that effect on her. So, breakfast first and in the restaurant for a change. All she had in her room was yoghurt and fruit and she needed more than that. Then she had a day to plan. Unless? She checked her phone. There was a notation against her texts.

Working until six on my own work. Hope you have a good day, see you later? P.s. that skirt needs to be preserved for posterity. That's posterity, not posterior.

She did laugh out loud at that and startled the three people waiting to get in as she got out.

Chapter Nine

Debra had a passion for lists. Her children howled and told her she was anal. Debra agreed with them amiably. So what? She liked to know what she had to do, what she wanted to do and also what she'd done.

The Hong Kong list was long and even though she'd managed to cross some things off and come to the conclusion some weren't important, there were still a fair few 'must dos' left. Once she ate what people would call a hearty breakfast and she called too much but enjoyed every mouthful, Debra went back to her room to decide on her plan for the day.

In the end it was no contest. She wanted to go to see the largest outdoor sitting Budda in the world, but wanted to be able to take her time.

She mentally calculated how long she realistically had before Braam might be free. Not long enough to go to Lantau by ferry, catch the bus to the Monastery, take her time in exploring and enjoy the meal she knew she could get there. Especially as she intended to come back down the hill by cable car before taking the MTR back to the hotel. There was an outside chance Braam might get finished earlier and she wanted to be handy. Not in the hotel exactly, but close enough to be around for whatever time he suggested. It was so against everything she'd ever done that the thought made her drop her pencil and list onto the floor.

Sap. Deb acknowledged that she, Debra Scotburn, was in way over her head and couldn't care less.

So, Sai Kung it was. Although the fishing village probably took nearly as long to get to, Debra had read enough to know she wouldn't spend as long looking around there as she would at the Monastery.

Twenty minutes later, having noted down her route, Debra was out in the hot air and on her way to the MTR station.

Lena and Kevan would be impressed with her use of public transport once they'd got over their 'oh good grief, is it safe'? worries. Role reversal but very reassuring — at times. Other times it made her want to scream. However, as Lena told her, now you know what it's like, Mum.

The worst of the queues to go through the ticket machines had died down and Debra was soon sitting on the train, reading her eBook and more than half in love with a hot sexy hero, who was a devil in more ways than one. By the time she got off the train and stood outside ready to catch the mini bus to her destination, she almost wished she could have stopped on the train and finished the story.

When her phone beeped, she was glad she hadn't. The text was from Braam. Debra felt like a silly teenager in the throes of her first romance. Don had made her heart beat faster, but this was so different. Not like a kid's crush, but deeper, harder and a lot more scary. At her age, disappointment would hit worse and last longer.

Now why had she thought of that?

Gah, deep and dark and doom and gloom. At this rate you'll have him married with a wife and six kids he's keeping secret. Get over it already. With that little pep talk given to herself, she looked at the text.

Hard at work, but with a grin on my face. About to have a video conference but wanted to say have a great day. Don't eat too much, we'll go out for dinner?

Debra got the gooey 'in so deep' sensation she had about Braam—when she stopped worrying.

Will do. See you later.

* * * *

Later, though, she wished someone was with her. It was a strange sensation. Usually she had no problems about being alone. In a lot of ways she preferred it. Selfish it might be, but Debra generally reveled in not having to consider anyone else when she made her plans.

She got off the bus and studied her map. Village was probably a misnomer—there was a lot of it and plenty was high density housing. However, she turned toward the water's edge and stopped dead, before she grinned in happiness. All along the seafront wall, little fishing boats were tied up, with people of all sizes and ages gutting their fish before they sold them.

Debra grabbed her camera and took a series of photos and hoped she'd gotten the progress from inquiry to purchase. Had Braam been here and done that? She shook her head at her stupidity. He lived in Hong Kong. He must have.

Maybe he'd do it with her? One day…

Hell, no more. Don't hatch your eggs and stuff. Wait and see.

People were hanging over the railings and shouting down their orders. Then the wrapped parcels were held up on poles in baskets and the money returned the same way. Every so often someone clambered up an iron ladder attached to the stone wall and shouted their wares. Well, Debra thought that was what was going on. In reality, she had no idea. They could be calling everyone tight fisted sods for all she knew. The sight was noisy, busy and colorful and she loved it. Her camera was used so much, it was a wonder it wasn't red hot. She would have to ask Braam what the protocol was here with regards to bartering and buying the day's catch.

One couple made her slow her steps and pause. Arm in arm, they were gesticulating at something in a boat moored below them and obviously had great bartering skills. The man pointed to something and shook his head. The woman gave a war cry and rolled her eyes.

"Go for it, Jack, show them how much you remember." She had an Australian twang and the sun-kissed skin of someone used to the tropical sun who took care not to burn. She looked up from the water and saw Debra nearby.

"Men — have to be macho and never admit they can't remember what they've learned. Ohh, woo hoo." She turned back to the man next to her who held a plastic bag high in the air. "He'll love you for that. Hell, I love you for it. Spot on." She kissed the man on the cheek and smiled at Debra as they walked off hand in hand away from the busy boats and restaurants.

Debra watched them go in a wistful mood. How nice that would have been if it were her and Braam. She'd bet he'd have been able to barter much more successfully.

Ah well, maybe one day. She pushed away the irritating thought that insisted on intruding into everything she enjoyed. The 'you're leaving soon, what then?' one. She wasn't going to think about that yet.

It's a holiday romance. A flirt-a-thon. Why didn't she believe that? *Because I don't want to. I want it to be more.*

The sun was hitting the sea and making the water sparkle. Without her sunglasses it would be too bright to see. She ambled in the opposite direction from the couple she'd envied. She'd find somewhere for a coffee and check out where to get a snack for later. And damn it she knew she'd check her texts and emails.

A few hundred yards on, the boats and fish sellers petered out and opposite the sea wall, restaurants lined the promenade. Several had tiers of tanks filled with swimming flapping fish all ready to be sacrificed for dinner. Gum-booted women jumped with effortless agility amongst them and pulled out the chosen fish to be cooked in their restaurant.

Waitrons smiled and entreated Debra to go into their restaurant, to try the day's special or perhaps sit and have a drink. With a smile, she declined them all. She wanted to wander through the tiny streets of the old village first. Otherwise she suspected she'd sit, people watch as she usually did and have to leave without seeing all she intended to. She passed a plaque, which had interesting tidbits about the old village then turned into a narrow lane. It was quiet, with most of the tarmac shaded by the houses that lined it on both sides. Halfway along, a couple of cafés vied with other. She chose the one on the left simply because an old man sitting at a table, eating dumplings and drinking tea out of an exquisite china lidded mug smiled at her. There were a few tables outside the narrow café front and one of those had the inevitable Mah Jong set ready for anyone who wanted to play.

Encouraged by the look of satisfaction of the old man as he sipped his drink, Debra ordered China tea rather than coffee. It was hot and this far back from the sea, the breeze had almost disappeared. The warm air was moved around by a large fan, which whirled from her to the old man and back again. Debra was glad of it, even if it didn't bring much coolth.

The tea was brought to her in a glass pot and she watched as the young waiter poured it into her cup with as much formality as if it was a full tea ceremony. He set the pot on the table, handed her a magazine and went to chat to his other customer.

Debra glanced at the magazine, turned it the other way up and looked again. Why when he'd spoken to her in English did he hand her a magazine in Chinese?

"Sorry."

The magazine was whisked from her fingers and another one dropped on the table next to her. That was better. It was a 'What's on in Hong Kong'? booklet. Debra took a sip of tea, gasped and waved her hand in front of her mouth. It was still too hot to drink. She checked the pages dedicated to that week, to see if there was anything that would interest her. Without looking toward the mug, Debra fumbled for it. As her hands closed around it, the waiter appeared, took it from her along with the teapot and disappeared inside. Across from her the old man moved with a speed that made her blink. For someone his age, he was incredibly agile. He had his plate of dumplings and his mug of tea in his hands as he followed the waiter into the café. A few seconds later the man reappeared and sat down at the table that had the Mah Jong set on it. The waiter came out of the café door like a jack-in-the-box, sat opposite him and rearranged the set to look as if they were mid game.

Debra sat opened mouth. What on earth? The waiter winked.

"Two minutes, ma'am. Please read." He looked pointedly at the booklet.

Intrigued and wondering what she'd gotten herself into, Debra did as he had asked.

A minute or so later—a minute that felt like ten—a couple wandered down the lane, stared at the three of them intently and said something to the waiter. He replied in short staccato bursts. The male of the couple seemed inclined to argue, but the woman took his arm and urged him away.

He turned to Debra. "You sit here to read?"

Behind him the waiter's eyes opened wide. A plea?

"It's very pleasant and I was hot. I needed a seat outside."

"And then she will come inside to have a drink," the waiter added.

Even though she was still bewildered, Debra thought it politic to agree.

"As he says," she said. "I'm looking forward to it." The expression of gratitude that the waiter flashed in her direction made her think she'd given the correct response. To whom and why she hoped she'd find out.

The visitor grunted and followed his colleague down the street and around the corner. As soon as they had disappeared, the waiter jumped up and went inside, appearing a few seconds later with a fresh pot of tea and a clean mug for Debra. She looked up at him and he smiled.

"Police. They're trying to stop people eating and drinking in the street in this old area. We say this is our land but...?" He shrugged. "There is, how do you say, an early warning system. They won't be back for at least an hour, so enjoy." He gave a quaint half bow and went back to where the old man was now eating his dumplings, even down to the one left mid bite, and placidly drinking tea. You would never have guessed that a few minutes before they had sat like actors in a very bad play.

Debra declined more tea, paid her bill and set off back toward the seafront and the restaurants. The whole episode had amused her. Did Braam know about...?

Enough. Give over now.

One restaurant had caught her eye. It advertised bite sized bliss. Although the description made her snigger, the idea of Chinese tapas sounded good. If there was anything nicer than being able to try lots of dishes, Debra hadn't found it. She bypassed a couple of other restaurants and smiled her 'no thanks' at the waitrons until she found the one she had noted. It was busy, but there was one table for two set next to the water and she made her way toward it. A smiling waitress picked up the unwanted place setting.

"Water and the Bliss special please." Debra knew exactly what she wanted. A clear head and some tasty snacks. Then she was going to walk back along the promenade and around the headland to look at the beach recommended in her guidebook. She might not have time to sit and enjoy its charms, but she wasn't going to miss it. A sandy beach was one thing she hadn't walked on for a while. Maybe she'd put some sand into a plastic bag as a memento.

Now that is silly. Maybe she'd be better off taking a selfie.

Before that, though, she had her lunch—albeit a late one—to enjoy. Within minutes the first dishes arrived. With each one, the waitress told her in Cantonese and English what it was. It reminded her of Braam and his attempts to teach her the basics. She dragged her mind back from Braam and what he might be doing and turned her attention to the food.

Every morsel was delicious and Debra had to remind herself over and over she was going out for dinner. Otherwise she suspected she could have sat and nibbled for hours. Eventually she put her chopsticks down. She had fumbled through the meal with them and wished she had her child's plastic Chopstick fastener to help out. But she wasn't going to accept failure and ask for a knife and fork.

She paid her remarkably modest bill and hunted down the communal loo, before she walked back past the few boats that hadn't managed to sell out of their fruits from the sea. It had amused her that several times, boats had drawn up near the restaurants to offload fresh supplies to the chefs. The sight of a man in white gumboots and a tall white hat, that he flapped in the air, arguing over the guard rails to someone you couldn't see, before hauling up a bag that moved, was one she'd never forget.

Her guidebook had waxed lyrical about the islands not far from the shore and especially about the one that had a golf course. As Debra walked away from the town, she reached the feet jetty for that island and stood open mouthed before she burst out laughing. The rules of golf and how to argue your way out of a bad shot were hilarious. She took a picture to send to her son. As a reasonably good golfer, he'd appreciate it.

The weather was made for dawdling, but Debra was conscious that time was passing. She didn't want to get caught up in the rush hour and she still held out the hope that Braam might be free earlier rather than later. Although when she reached the beach she wished she could linger.

It was idyllic, although certainly not private. Definitely no chance to get up to anything remotely personal. However, the few canoes, several dragon boats and a couple of rowing boats bobbed gently on the soft swell and created a beautiful picture. Maybe if Braam had a day off before she left she'd ask him to come back here with her.

With a sigh, Debra turned and retraced her steps toward the town and the bus station.

It was typical that she saw the bus depart as she approached the bus stance. A quick check of the timetable showed there wasn't another one due for several minutes. She stood behind a few other people who hadn't made it in time, took out her phone and checked if she had any messages. The screen was blank and she hadn't. Should she text Braam?

No acting needy. He said he was going to be busy. Instead she sent a 'having a great time' text to her children. The green minibus turned up before her resolve broke and she sent a message to Braam. She was *not* needy.

In the short time she'd waited, a queue had formed behind her and as soon as the driver opened his door they all moved forward. Debra got on, scanned her Oyster card and grabbed a seat. In theory, no one should stand, but in practice it didn't always work. However, just in case, she wasn't going to be the one who was turfed off.

The minibus set off with a lurch and a judder and the driver drove out of the bus station like he had an inspector on his tail. Maybe he had, but if so there was no chance the bus would be caught. It weaved in and out of the numerous bicycles that straggled over the road and over took cars and lorries with a blare of the horn.

The woman next to Debra gave a gasp and her lips moved, even though she uttered no words. If she was praying Debra hoped she'd be included in the plea for a safe journey. By the time the bus drew up outside the MTR station, with a jolt that had most people sliding to the edge of their seats, Debra felt sick. She was thankful they had arrived there on one piece. Everyone said the Italians were fast drivers. This guy could give them a run for their money.

The woman next to her harangued the driver as they got off. He shrugged and once the last person who wanted to leave had left the vehicle he set off in exactly the same way they'd arrived. Too fast and with a squeal of brakes.

Debra walked into the train station and wondered how she'd managed the journey without being ill.

An hour later, she was hot, grumpy and ready for a swim. The train had been packed, the man who almost stood on her toes sweated profusely and the woman next to her had obviously had an excess of garlic in her meal. The scents of hot bodies, garlic and Hong Kong had vied with each other and the over-worked air conditioning didn't have a chance. Debra took out a tissue and pretended to blow her nose. Then she sat with her hand propped on her knee and the tissue over her lower face. She could cope with anything in small doses. This wasn't one. The train got busier the nearer they got to Hong Kong Island and by the time she needed to get off, Debra had a pounding headache. The swim looked more and more inviting by the minute.

For the first time since she'd arrived in Hong Kong, she didn't enjoy the walk back to the hotel from the MTR station. Rush hour had commenced with a vengeance and people dashed about knocking her and each other. Pain pummeled into her head like a blacksmith's hammer on an anvil and the scents and smells of the street vendors cooking made her feel more than slightly nauseated. She reached the doors of the hotel and smiled wanly at the doorman. The cool, dim light in the foyer was as welcome as a major win on the lottery. Debra gulped the chilly air gratefully. Had she had too much sun?

She didn't think so. It was probably lack of water, sore feet and a need to see Braam.

Braam. Try as she might, Debra couldn't help her heart beating that little bit faster. It had been a strange experience, looking around somewhere and wanting to share that experience.

At the far side of the foyer she noticed Braam standing next to one of the men who tended the plants in the indoor garden. As ever, Braam was dressed in a dark suit and white shirt and Debra shivered in a good way at the sight. Would she ever not go weak at the knees when she saw him? She hoped not. It was juice-inducing pleasure. It was so good to see him. Debra started to walk past the lifts and toward him, at the same time as the lift doors opened and the girl she'd seen at Sai Kung bartering for fish came out.

She walked past Debra without a second glance and made a beeline for Braam. Debra stopped walking as the woman broke into a run and hurled herself into Braam's arms.

"Braam, oh, my God, Braam, we did it." She flung her arms around Braam, hugged him and started to cry.

Debra watched. Fascinated and with a strange feeling of foreboding in her stomach. A heavy, leaden, gut-churning sensation that crawled over her skin, as Braam hugged the woman and stroked her hair.

"What, love? Shhhh, calm down, we can sort it, don't worry." The tone of Braam's voice told Debra he was worried. "Tell me."

"We're having a baby," the woman said. Her words floated clearly back to Debra. "Two babies, in fact. Oh, Braam, we're going to have twins. Be parents and a real family."

"What?" As Debra watched and wondered if it was a nightmare and she'd wake up in her bed with Braam next to her, Braam grinned and high-fived the air.

"Woo hoo, oh yeah." Braam swung the woman around in a circle, unheeding of any watchers. "Oh my. Two. Mummy, Daddy and their twins. Yes, oh, God, baby, that is amazing. You're amazing. Damn, I wish I'd been with you when you found out."

A strange buzzing noise sounded in Debra's ears as she watched the couple as they exchanged a loving kiss and shattered her world.

She didn't move toward them. Instead she stood behind a topiary bush, which was bizarrely cut into the shape of a temple. Strange the things you noticed when seconds before your life had been changed forever.

"Do you need to sit down? Drink milk or whatever? We need to celebrate." His voice carried clearly across the foyer.

Debra glanced at the woman's tear-streaked, but happy face and at the ear-to-ear grin on Braam's.

"Parents. Orange juice, that's it, and, well... Oh, God, I'm babbling. Come on." Braam took the arm of the woman and walked toward to the lifts. "Hold on, what's that by the plants?" He moved in Debra's direction.

She had to get away. Without looking in their direction again, Debra headed for the other bank of lifts and prayed that one would be waiting. Her luck was in. Within seconds she was inside and pressing the floor button. The lift didn't move.

Come on, come on, ah, shit and fuck. She wrenched open her bag to get out her room key. In her agitation, she'd forgotten she needed to swipe it over the security panel to make the lift move.

Where's the fucking key? Her heart beat erratically and her pulse jumped like a flea in a circus as she hunted. *Think, woman, it's in here somewhere.* Debra rummaged amongst the guidebooks, sun cream, tissues and whatever else lurked in her bag, before she remembered she'd put the swipe card into the zippered pocket in the lining of the bag. Then it took seconds to retrieve it, use it and set the lift in motion.

The feeling of upwards movement usually made her sway and feel hollow. Not this time. This time she was too busy controlling her erratic breathing to notice anything else. Her mind whirled. *Who's the woman? How can Braam behave as he has? Why isn't the woman sharing his suite? What the hell does this make me?*

Cuckolded. The old-fashioned word popped into her mind and stuck there. Even though it wasn't meant for a woman—it meant a man who was the husband of an adulteress—Debra couldn't get it out of her head. She had no idea what, if anything, described her position, except maybe stupid, naive, gullible... The list of those sorts of words was endless.

The lift stopped at her floor and the doors opened. Debra looked out into the corridor somewhat warily. After all she'd seen the woman there earlier, with a man. So who was the man?

There was no one around. Debra left the lift and hurried toward her room. As she passed the other lifts, she saw the indicator showing that one was on its way upward. She'd never managed to swipe her key card and get inside her suite so fast in her life.

Once she had shut the door behind her, Debra lay back on it and panted. It was so stupid. Why was she hiding as if *she* had done something wrong? She hadn't come on to someone else whilst she was in a relationship. Or about to be a parent.

"Bit on the side," Debra said out loud. "Get used to it. Floozy." She grimaced. "No, not a floozy, just an idiot who fell for the oldest trick in the book." She pushed herself off the door, walked across to the bed and dropped her bag onto it. The now smoothed and pristine coverlet reminded her of how crumpled a bed could get and in spite of her misery and anger, her pussy contracted. It had been spectacular sex.

Do not think about sex, woman. No sex, no hanky panky, no fathers to be. Nothing. Pure as the driven snow from now on. Buy a new rabbit and call it Hector or something. Do not think about dishy Dutch/Portuguese/Chinese/English or whatever two-faced, two timing security assholes. However, that was easier said than done.

Debra turned on the shower and stood under it until the tension had left her. Then she wrapped a towel around herself and wondered what next?

Braam was supposed to take her out for dinner. How could he now? A sudden thought struck her. What if the woman knew? What if they liked that sort of thing? Betrayal and— *No, do not go there.* Debra knew anything slightly less than all above board, ordinary sex wasn't for her.

Define ordinary? Oh shut up, mind, I know what I mean. But did she?

"No threesomes, no cheating and no jaggy implements," she said out loud and got off the bed to get dressed. "And an explanation."

As she was certain that there would be no romantic, intimate dinner for two, Debra pulled on a pair of casual trousers and a top and looked into the fridge. She'd manage to find something to eat, even if it wasn't with fine wines and by candlelight.

The doorbell rang as she opened her laptop to check her emails and Debra glanced at the clock. Too early for it to be Braam, if he actually bothered to turn up. Had she forgotten to put the 'do not disturb' light on again? She walked to the door and checked the peephole. It *was* Braam and the bastard looked the same hot, sexy man as ever. Debra took a deep breath and put her hand over her heart for a brief moment. *Play it cool.* She took off the safety chain and opened the door. Braam leaned in the doorjamb and smiled. The smile might do stupid things to her insides, but Debra noticed it didn't reach his eyes. They were cool and wary.

"You're early." She stood back to let him go past her into the room. He didn't move.

"Yeah. Well, I've come to say I won't be able to manage dinner tonight. Something's come up." His voice was low and he half shrugged.

Well, something certainly did. Your fucking cock in her pussy, you bastard.

"Yes?" She spoke with a query in her voice.

"Yes."

"Oh, dear. Well it's obviously something you can't—" or won't her tone implied—"discuss."

"No, er, yes. Well, no, I can't discuss it. It's not up to me and well. Oh, shit, I'm sorry, Deb. I'll do my best to get away early and come up and explain. Okay?"

"Yes." If he could be brief so could she. Debra held onto the edge of the door and hoped her white-knuckled grip didn't show. It was either that or shout, scream, throw things, or maybe just fall down and cry. She'd never let a man see her cry over him before and she had no intention of starting now. "If you can't, don't worry. I'll wash my hair and paint my nails."

"Right." He obviously didn't understand the sarcasm. "Then, er, if I don't get back, I'll see you tomorrow around seven?"

"Yeah."

Braam hesitated then moved away from the doorjamb.

"But I need this to keep me going." He leaned forward and prized her hand off the door. "I need to feel you and be held." Braam pulled her close and before Debra had time to remonstrate, he was kissing her. He teased her lips with his tongue and demanded entry to her mouth and stroked her cheek with one long finger. Debra melted. That single finger on her skin scorched her, branded her and held her in thrall.

When he trailed his hand down her spine, she shivered and gasped at the red-hot sensations that skittered behind it and into her core. The caress on her bum made her squirm. The tiny delve into the crease of her ass made her gasp and the triumphant sound he made—almost a groan—made her pussy damp.

"Oh, God, I need..." The sound of the lift doors opening filtered into the sexual haze that surrounded her. It seemed it had the same effect on Braam who pulled back abruptly. At least he looked as dazed as Debra felt.

"Shit, right, well." He ran his hand over his hair. "I'm sorry, I need to dash. I'll speak to you tomorrow. Shit, Deb, I'm so sorry." He turned and walked down the corridor at a pace that made Debra feel giddy.

Chapter Ten

A good crying jag might make you feel like crap, but it had to be beneficial, surely? Not for the bloated face, red-rimmed eyes and the hollow tummy. But to get it out of your system, stop being sorry for yourself and get mad.

However, telling yourself something and acting on it wasn't the same. Or as easy. Deb looked around the room and felt sick. What fool's paradise had she been living in?

The room now seemed sordid. The pictures on the wall that a few days previously she'd thought charming mocked her and it was all she could do not to turn them to face the wall. She had to get away. Home, anywhere as long as it was away.

That wasn't as easy as she had hoped. There wasn't a seat on a London bound plane vacant that night. The standby list was overflowing and the next couple of nights were no better. It looked like the only definite flight home was the one she was booked on. Debra hated the sensation of spiders crawling over her skin and butterflies in her stomach that attacked her. There was no way she could stay in Hong Kong and not go head to head with Braam over his perfidy and she couldn't allow herself to do it. There was a pregnant woman now in the equation who was blameless and didn't need all the grief that would surely hit her. Debra knew herself well enough to know if she began she would go way over the top and not mince her words.

"Where do you have a flight to?" she asked. "I need a break." Goodness knew if the woman thought she was deranged, or running to—or from—her lover. Debra didn't much care.

An hour later and a sizeable amount added to her credit card, Debra packed her belongings. She'd gotten onto a plane for Singapore due to leave at the unhealthy hour of one thirty a.m., booked herself three nights in a hotel—not a Channing hotel—and planned her getaway. All she had to do was get out of the hotel and to the airport. She wasn't going to check out, because after all the room was hers for another four nights if you counted the one she was in. She could pay her bill online, at the appropriate time. Her story was ready—'off to see a friend for a night or so'—if she needed it, but with luck she wouldn't.

The contents of her fridge made an unusual meal. The pâté, crackers and grapes would make a handy snack if she needed one. The chicken curry and rice she heated and ate while she planned her timings. Debra often commented that caution was best and this time she knew it was. She'd head out earlier than needed. After all, she'd sprung for a business class seat, knowing that she'd be able to then use the executive lounge if she arrived early. By eight p.m. she'd left her room and was hauling her suitcase along the corridor. As ever at that time of night, it was deserted, which she'd reckoned would be the case.

She took a deep breath and called for the lift.

Her luck was in and she made it all the way to the door of the hotel without seeing anyone except the doorman.

"You checking out, Mrs. Scotburn?" Was he inquisitive or the normal conversation? "You need me call you a taxi for the airport station?"

"Oh, no, I'm off to see a friend for a couple of days. I don't go home for a week or so yet."

Liar, liar, pants on fire. "I'll have a taxi, though, to the levels. She said she'd come for me, but what's the point, eh?"

He shrugged and darted out into the middle of the main road to wave at every taxi that went past.

Debra began to sweat as the minutes ticked by. She was about to say 'don't bother, I'll walk to the MTR' when one swerved over two lanes of traffic and pulled up with a screech of brakes.

The doorman smiled in a relieved way and loaded her suitcase into the boot.

"See you in a couple of days?"

Debra nodded. "Yeah, this is too good a chance to miss."

The doorman held her door open. "Good show. Great news for Braam, eh? He said you and he were old friends."

So that's what he called us. Shit, does everyone know? What must they think of me? She smiled. "The best. She looks radiant."

"Been a long time coming. The levels, lady tell you where." He spoke to the driver and banged on the roof. "Enjoy, ma'am."

The car pulled away so fast, Debra reckoned half the tire rubber was left behind them. The way the driver wove in and out of the cars made her wonder if he was any relation to the bus driver of the previous day.

"Whereabouts, ma'am?"

She'd concentrated so hard on ignoring the traffic, she'd forgotten that she hadn't said where. Her mind went blank. "Oh, er, at the bottom of the Central Escalator will be perfect." She could walk or get another cab from there. The driver grunted. It would be good and central for him and he'd pick another fare up there much more easily than in an obscure residential area.

Debra paid him, took her suitcase and walked toward the footbridge that took you up to the escalator. And turned in the opposite direction. Toward the MTR airport express. She'd even be in plenty of time to check her luggage in there instead of lugging it all the way to the airport. She didn't know if you could do that anywhere else in the world but it was brilliant.

The aerial walkway about the busy streets was a godsend. Now she was away from the hotel, Debra was in no hurry. She meandered along and people-watched. It was busy, even though for Hong Kong it was too early for most people to be out and about.

At one intersection below, cars were backed up and the tooting of horns made several people go to the wall and look over. Debra joined them and chuckled at the sight of a lorry, which had somehow got itself stuck across the road. The driver gesticulated out of the window and shouted at several bystanders who seemed to be more of a hindrance than a help.

The onlookers from the walkway shouted down and added their suggestions and Debra stood back to listen. Not many of the comments were in English, but in whatever language, their meaning was clear. The driver was an idiot. She got the impression he'd be stuck there for a fair while. A police car drew up with its light flashing and two policemen got out, to point, blow whistles and try to make sense of the mayhem.

With a grin and the happiest she'd been since she'd seen Braam and his—his what?—Debra turned away and stared down toward the intersection. There was a couple that looked... She hid behind a tall man wearing a shocking pink tracksuit and bright green trainers and stared as best she could around him.

It was Braam and he was arm in arm with the pregnant 'ohh, Braam, we're having twins' woman. Debra ducked backwards as he looked up and recognition showed on his face.

Debra didn't wait to see what happened next. Grateful for the fact that she was wearing trainers, she moved to the far side of the walkway and jogged away with her suitcase bobbing behind her.

It took less than five minutes to reach the station and to her relief there was no queue at the check-in desk. Half an hour later she sat on the train to the airport. She felt she'd run a marathon in bare feet and been told she'd been disqualified and needed to do it all over again. This skulking about was not good for the nerves.

* * * *

"Braam, are you listening? I said I wish Jack could have joined us. Damned crisis and the oil industry. I was so looking forward to the fish he bartered for. You should have seen him, he was a star. All

Cantonese and arm waving. He fell in twice and the fish nibbled his dick."

"That's good, I knew it would... Eh?" Braam looked away from the walkway and stared at her. "Kris, you what?"

"Ha." She sounded triumphant. "I knew you weren't listening. So, you gonna tell me what's up your arse or not?"

He sighed. He should be over the moon and all he could think of was how he'd screwed up. He should have explained to Debra why he'd canceled their date, not say he'd tell her later. Why had he acted like a horse's backside? Because he wasn't used to explaining himself was no excuse. Even though Kris had asked him not to say anything until later. That of course had gone to hell in a hand basket when Jack had told every one of the hotel's staff. Braam had excused himself from the celebrations and rung Debra's room, only to hear the phone ring out and not be answered. Before he had the chance to try to find her, Jack had received his crisis phone call and disappeared.

"Nothing's up my arse, as you so elegantly call it." Even to himself he didn't sound convincing. Had it been Debra? She wasn't in view now. If it was her, what was she doing in Central at this time of the evening?

"Of course not. And I lied. I'm expecting quins. Fess up, this is me. I know you." She poked him in the ribs. Her fingers might be slim and elegant, but they could deliver a good sharp poke.

Braam winced theatrically and she grinned. "You've screwed up and daren't admit it."

"Kris, you're crazy."

"Braam, so are you if you think I'm buying that nothing crap. Tell me."

"Yeah, okay, once we sit down." He urged her toward the restaurant he'd chosen for their celebration once he knew it was only the two of them to celebrate. Once they were seated inside the Michelin starred establishment and their order taken, Kris turned to him.

"Talk."

"You don't half nag, you know."

"I know." Kris sounded smug. "Jack tells me that all the time."

Braam ruffled her hair and she squealed. He laughed as her good humor rubbed off on him. "My brother the henpecked husband, eh?"

"Ha, not a chance. Your brother gives as good as he gets." His sister-in-law rubbed her tummy and winked. "Hence twins."

Braam choked on his water. In deference to Kris' condition, he hadn't ordered any alcohol and said they'd toast her pregnancy with sparkling water. "How on earth does he cope?"

"Very well. Now enough stalling. Is it a woman?"

Trust Kris to go straight to the point.

"Yeah, and I think I've been very stupid."

"You're a man, it goes with the territory." Kris sat back in her chair and waited until the waiter had put warming trays on the table and described the dishes they were about to eat. "Okay, spill the beans. Who is she, where is she, what is she and why didn't you invite her to come out with us?" Kris waved her chopsticks at him. "You ashamed of us?"

"Don't be daft. But you said it was all hush-hush."

"And I burst into tears all over you in the foyer and told you there and then Jack told the world and his wife. Not much hush-hush about it after that, was there? So?" She stared at him until Braam was sure he blushed.

So, he felt like he'd been rapped over the knuckles.

"Yeah, well." *Blimey I sound like a sulky schoolboy who's been caught out copying his homework or something.*

"Braam Van Meister, there's no yeah well about it. What did you, or more to the point, didn't you do?"

He pushed his plate of food to one side and traced circles on the tablecloth with his chopsticks. The thought of eating any more made him nauseated.

"I told her I couldn't see her tonight. But didn't say why. I told her that I'd try to get up to see her later on. Okay, don't look at me as if I've crawled out from under a stone. What else could I say?"

"That your brother and his wife had arrived unexpectedly and did she want to come out to dinner with us all perhaps?" Kris shook her head. "What's hard about that?"

Put like that, nothing.

"I admit I fucked up."

"You so did and if your lady is anything of a woman that's the last fucking you'll be doing for a long while. Get ready to grovel, Braam. Big time mega groveling."

"Krista Van Meister, what would your husband say if he caught you using language like that?"

Kris giggled. "That I was right and suggest I wash my mouth out. So, what are you going to do? You have to go and see her and tell her what the hell was in your pea brain." She waved her hand in the air and a waiter approached. "Braam, get it in a doggie bag. Then we can take it back and invite your lady to share it with us. Maybe then she'll accept what an arse you are, but you're so in love you couldn't help it."

Whoa... Braam dipped his head in acknowledgment. She was right on every count. Whoever said love couldn't hit you hard and fast was wrong. He asked for their food to be bagged and made rapid apologies about having to get back to the hotel. As he was a regular at the restaurant and they knew him well, there was no problem in agreeing to his request. Within a few minutes he'd paid the bill, got the food and he and Kris were in a taxi, which the restaurant had called for them.

The traffic did its usual stop-start routine as they inched toward Causeway Bay. It was typical Hong Kong evening driving conditions, but now he was going to be able to explain and apologize for being an arse, Braam could almost believe it was slower than usual.

"Come on, come on, move into the other lane and let us through." He muttered under his breath as a double decker bus straddled two lanes and they became stuck behind it. "Seriously, what is it with bus drivers?"

Kris touched his arm. "Braam, it's trying to turn right. Calm down. We'll get there when we get there."

"She didn't answer the phone when I rang her room earlier on," Braam told her.

"Ah."

How on earth could that one word convey so much?

"She probably went out for a walk or something," Kris said and hugged his arm. "You know, to calm down and not break anything. And she'll be back and ready to listen."

She didn't sound convinced. Nor was he.

The bus finally moved away and the taxi shot into the gap like a hound out of a trap. Kris slid forward on the seat and Braam clamped her to his side.

"Whoa, I have to look after you until Jack gets back. No falling on your knees."

She laughed. "Not much likelihood of that. Right, now we're here, you go and find your lady. What's she called, by the way?"

"Debra." He paid the driver and helped Kris out.

"Debra. Then give me a ring if you want me to join you. Otherwise I'll see you at breakfast." Kris stood on tiptoe and kissed him on the cheek. "Good luck and remember to grovel. Look, the flower shop's still open." She walked into the hotel.

Braam watched her head for the lifts and stared at the florist's window. Was it too twee to take flowers as an apology? The worst she could do was to throw them at him. He went inside and spent a precious few minutes choosing some blooms, before he headed back to the hotel.

The doorman held the door open for him.

"Aww, Braam, you shouldn't have." The guy winked. "Though I do have a soft spot for tulips."

Braam shook his head as he walked into the foyer. "Howard, I'll tell your wife."

"She knows. Hey, if they're for Mrs. Scotburn, you missed her by a couple of minutes."

Braam stopped mid stride and turned around. His skin crawled. "Pardon?"

"Mrs. Scotburn. I called her a taxi earlier. To go to her friend's. I asked if she was checking out and she said no."

The sense of relief was so intense, Braam had the silly thought that it was a wonder he didn't have a speech bubble coming out of his head saying 'phew'.

"Damn, I thought I'd catch her before she went. Ah well, I'll have them put in her room for her."

The doorman nodded. "Shame, though. They'll be past their best when she gets back."

What? There was no way he could question Howard and not have the whole hotel wonder what had happened. He knew that even though they hadn't broadcast their friendship, the interaction between Debra and himself had been closely monitored.

"True, but at least she'll know I did my best. I hoped I'd be back in time."

Howard inclined his head in agreement. "She was mighty pleased about your news, though. Said Mrs. Jack looked radiant."

Oh, fuck and shit. Now he was well and truly in the mire. Braam knew enough about women to know Debra would be hurt as well as pissed off. As for meeting friends? Who were they? More to the point, where were they?

He entered the lift and pressed the button for Debra's floor. If she wasn't there—and, of course, why would Howard say she wasn't if she was?—then a little illegal breaking and entering might be on the cards.

He didn't need to be illegal. As he approached Debra's door, he saw it was open. His pulse jumped and his mouth became dry with worry, excitement, he wasn't sure which. Was she back?

It seemed not. The chambermaid was in the middle of the evening bed turn down service.

The disappointment hit him like a fist in the gut.

The young girl looked up at him as she smoothed the coverlet. "Oh my, they're lovely. Mrs. Scotburn will adore them. Mind you, I wondered for a minute if she'd checked out and no one told me."

Braam smiled noncommittally. "No, she's gone to see friends."

"Ah." The maid nodded and straightened up. "That accounts for her stuff missing then. I did wonder. Er, if you're going to arrange those," she pointed to the flowers, "can I let you shut the door behind you? I know it's maybe not quite what we're supposed to do but..." Her voice trailed off.

Braam smiled and hoped it looked reassuring and not as if he was going to an execution. "Of course. I'll put them where she'll see them and get off to my office." He opened the cupboard under the compact kitchen sink and took out the crystal vase that every suite was equipped with. The chambermaid left the room and Braam let out the breath he hadn't been conscious he held. It took scant moments to put the flowers in the vase. He was no flower arranger, but the perfume surely made up for any deficiency in the display? The heady scent of the flowers filled the room and he sniffed appreciatively. Now he had to hope she wasn't allergic to pollen or whatever. He scribbled a note and sealed it in one of the envelopes provided. As he was about to leave the room, Braam remembered the chambermaid's words. *Stuff missing?* His skin tingled and he couldn't help but feel as if he was committing some great crime as he opened the bathroom door.

It was as impersonal as any unoccupied hotel room. The towels were folded neatly on their shelves, the toiletries aligned perfectly and the bathmat placed over the side of the bath. There was no makeup, no perfume or sponge bag. Nothing to show the room was occupied. With a growing sense of panic and a premonition that he'd blown it, Braam left the bathroom, walked into the bedroom and opened the wardrobe.

The hotel bathrobe hung neatly on a padded hanger and the complimentary slippers were in their bag on the shelf next to them. The iron and ironing board were where they should be. The row of hangers hung neatly, side by side—with no clothes on them. The leaden lump in his stomach grew larger as Braam slid open the other wardrobe door. The one that had the safe in.

The door open, empty, safe.

She's gone. Fuck and shit, what have I done? Braam shut the wardrobe door slowly and felt tears prickle his eyes. Why on earth had he held back? Why hadn't he explained? Oh it was easy to blame Kris and say she didn't want the news broadcast, but hell, she'd shrieked it all over the foyer.

Braam walked around the compact suite. Debra had left nothing. Not even a hairgrip or a lipstick lid. No scent of her remained. He wondered if he pinched himself he'd wake up and find it was all a hot, heavy dream?

Had she known something when he'd cried off their date? Now he thought about it in detail, she had looked pale, but he'd put it down to the lighting in the hallway. Had she heard about his impending uncle-hood? However, he couldn't fathom why she'd run when she'd heard he was going to be an uncle. Surely the fact that he hadn't mentioned it then broken their date wasn't such a crime to make her leave? Braam circled the rooms once more, even though he knew he'd find nothing. It was as if she'd never been there. What was it the chambermaid had said? She wondered if Debra had checked out and she hadn't been notified? Surely not. There was no way Braam was going to ask. Thankfully he wouldn't have to. At least he could use his security codes to scan the residents' lists.

He checked you could clearly see his note propped next to the flowers and left the room to head up to his own quarters. As he waited for the ascending lift, the one next to it, which had descended, stopped and the doors opened. Kris got out and blinked when she saw him.

"Hey, you looking for me? I went up to the walking track. It's so pretty."

Braam sighed. "Nah, sorry. I was looking for my lady. She's gone."

"Pardon?"

The lift he called arrived and Kris took his arm and dragged him inside. She used her key, pressed his floor button and stared at him as they went upwards.

"Explain that little statement, Braam. What do you mean she's gone? Gone how? For food? For a walk? Off you? Now after your numpty act, I can understand that one."

"I wish that's all it was. She's left the hotel. I've put the flowers in her room and all her stuff was gone."

"Her room? On the floor I'm staying on?"

"Yeah, why. What does it matter?"

"Curvy? Dark hair, gray eyes and about my height?"

"That's her. She told Howard she'd gone to see friends."

"There you are then." Kris towed him across from the lift to his door. "Open this."

In spite of his misery, Braam was amused. When did his sister-in-law get so bossy? He opened the door and stood back to let her precede him. Once they were in his suite, Kris filled the kettle and switched it on.

"Talk."

"I don't know where to start," he said honestly. "I went and bought flowers and then Howard said she was away for... Hold on, let me think." He replayed the conversation he'd had with the doorman. "He said, as I best I can remember, that I'd missed her by minutes. Howard had gotten her a taxi and she'd said she wasn't checking out, she was going to visit friends. And she agreed how lovely your news was."

Kris handed him a cup of tea.

The fragrant scent made his tummy rumble. Maybe they'd heat their food up soon.

"My news?" Kris said. "Or did she think it was your news? Seeing that after I'd done my squeal and told the world about the babies, I could have sworn I saw her near the lifts. I noticed her because I think she was near Jack and I when he was doing his arm waving, fish bartering act in Sai Kung. We snickered about macho men."

"Why would she think it was...? Ah, I see. Oh, fuck."

Kris bit her lip. "Yeah. I said at the top of my voice that we were going to become parents. I didn't say Jack and I, or that you were going to be an uncle. I was so damned excited, that I blurted it out without thinking. Now to anyone who doesn't know Jack, or me, that could be a natural assumption to make. I've gone and messed things up, haven't I?" She swiped at her eyes, grabbed a tissue from the box on the work surface and blew her nose.

As much as he wanted to disagree, there wasn't much he could say. However, he tried. "We both did, I guess. I didn't explain why I was canceling because I wanted to check with you two if it was okay to tell Deb. Then I was going to go back, explain and ask her to join us for a drink. But, if she overheard you, why on earth didn't she confront me with what she'd heard? Ask me what the hell I was playing at? Why are you looking at me as if I have two heads?"

The pity and scorn mixed in Kris' expression were enough to make his skin tighten in a not very pleasant way.

"Oh, come on, Braam. Think on. If you were a woman, who had thought she was on the verge of something special and discovered it looked like the guy wasn't purely a lying, cheating bastard, but his wife was pregnant, you might want to cut his balls off. But you'd never confront him if there was a chance you were going to upset that pregnant woman. You'd wait and decide what to do. Maybe she's gone to friends until she sorts her head out. Then she'll come and confront you."

All of a sudden Braam didn't feel hungry anymore.

Chapter Eleven

The flight was on time leaving and landed early. The hotel was all she could have asked for and more and her room was ready. Debra wandered round it aimlessly and unpacked the bare necessities. She wasn't in Singapore for more than a few days and it wasn't worth doing anything else. For the umpteenth time she asked herself why she'd left Hong Kong and not tried to speak to Braam alone.

Because it would crucify me. Oh, grow up. She chastised herself. *It's a two-faced cheating bloke and a holiday fling. That's it. Build a bridge and get over it.* The problem was that saying it was one thing, believing it was another. Debra was hurting.

It's happened to people before you, it'll happen to people after. It's life. It's his poor wife I'm sorry for. Does she know she's got a sleep-around rat for a husband? Debra bit back a sob and bit her lip hard. Even after seeing and hearing the evidence, she still found it hard to equate Braam with a man who would cheat on anyone.

She brushed her hair and looked at herself in the mirror. What a mess. It was a wonder they hadn't asked for a doctor's certificate before they let her fly. She was gray under her tan, her eyes were dull and her usually shiny hair seemed lank. Debra shook her head.

"Enough already," she said out loud. "No man's worth more than a day of moping. I've got a city to discover again."

With that motivational speech in mind, Debra took herself into the shower and by the time she emerged pink skinned and squeaky clean, she *was* in a much better mood. As she emerged from the hotel into the heat, she took a deep breath and smelled the mixture of cooking, seawater and hot air that spelled the tropics to her.

A few feet away, the river ran past the hotel, with tour boats and ferries crisscrossing past her. Debra turned toward the harbor to reacquaint herself with the Merlion, the half mermaid, half lion statue that was the symbol of Singapore. It was several years since she'd visited and the skyline was considerably changed. It had been one of the places she'd not visited on her year away. Some cities had to be missed out and Singapore was one of them. However, it seemed she found herself here after all. Watching children laughing and running round the statue and its tiny 'baby', Debra was so glad she'd managed a visit, even if it was for all the wrong reasons. She'd enjoy her stay, head back to Hong Kong in time for her flight to the UK and reflect on her holiday romance. Then she'd decide what the next phase of her life would be.

First, though, she'd take a wander up the quayside toward a coffee shop she remembered and sit and watch the world go by.

The shops and the office buildings were a mixture of old and new and Debra took her time as she remembered an old traditional restaurant then saw a new skyscraper a few streets away. Sandwiched in between a bar and a shuttered shop front, a narrow staircase led toward 'massages' and she remembered her husband's amusement at the names of some of the businesses. She stood still for a moment, closed her eyes and let the essence of Singapore sink into her. If Hong Kong was her favorite city in the world, Singapore came a close second.

The sound of a cycle bell made her move in a hurry. A man pushing a handcart hurried past her, ringing the bell furiously. He smiled and nodded and Debra grinned back. Innovation was definitely the key.

Not far ahead, the river curved in an elegant arc with a wide bridge over it. Debra crossed halfway over the bridge and turned to look back down the river in the direction she had walked from. From here you got a whole new perspective of all the new buildings that dotted along the harbor and the coast.

Over on Sentosa Island, buildings seemed to have sprung up like a rash and Debra stared. One logo on a building either on the island or nearby looked awfully familiar. It was too far away to see clearly, but she'd bet her hard sought after happy mood it said Channing.

Damn, blast and bugger. I will not let it bother me. She turned her back and resolutely walked toward her destination. She wouldn't think about the fact it would be in her vision when she retraced her steps. A good cup of coffee and a snack and she could ignore it.

To her surprise, she did exactly that. A few hours later, as she sat by the infinity pool on the third floor of the hotel and looked out over the river, Debra acknowledged that leaving and putting space between her and Braam had been the right thing to do. Maybe one day she'd email him via the hotel and say... She chortled inwardly. Say what? Hi, remember me? I'm the woman you screwed when your wife was pregnant. Or maybe 'one of the women...'

No more of that. Debra took out the what's-on leaflet she'd picked up from her room and scanned the pages. Maybe she'd get the cable car over to Sentosa Island from Mount Faber and do the whole tourist and man-made beach experience for a day. And if she saw a Channing hotel, she would ignore it.

With her mind made up, Debra went for a lazy swim. The pool area was empty except for a couple who sat at the other end of the water, each reading a book, sipping wine and nibbling on a plate of snacks.

By the time she'd hung over the infinity pool edge and watched the ferries stopping down below, Debra was ready for something to eat herself. She got out, wrapped herself in her robe, stretched out on her sun lounger and read the poolside menu.

As if he was a mind reader, a waiter appeared and within ten minutes she was eating samosas and sipping her own glass of wine. She opened her eReader and pulled up a thriller about St Andrews she'd begun to read on the plane from Hong Kong.

As the afternoon wore on, clouds that grew steadily thicker obscured the sun. A breeze teased the bushes that were dotted around the area and the pool boy immediately started to close and secure the sun umbrellas.

"Storm coming in," he said. "Won't last long, but I reckon it'll be heavy. You'll be glad you're back at the hotel."

Debra took the hint and gathered up her things. Even before she'd reached the door to go inside, he'd lifted the mattress and stored it under cover. By the time she reached her room, the rain was rattling the windows of the executive floor lounge and the quayside was a sea of colorful umbrellas. Several had already been blown inside out.

Debra shivered, even though she wasn't cold, and opened her door.

She'd been lucky with her room, which had a balcony overlooking the river and enough of a roof to allow her to open the doors and look out at the wet and windswept scene without getting wet or windswept. She made a cup of tea and drank it as the clouds scudded past.

Half an hour later she admitted defeat and stretched out on the bed. Last night's lack of sleep had caught up with her. There was time for a nap before cocktails in the lounge.

To be on the safe side, she set her alarm and closed her eyes.

* * * *

The soft stroke up and down her arm made Debra purr with pleasure. She wriggled and he laughed softly before he blew gently in her ear, nipped the lobe with his teeth and kissed the soft skin of her nape.

Debra moaned. That erotic nip and suck made her pussy damp and her inner muscles contract.

"Braam?"

He moved his head so she could see the wicked gleam in his blue eyes. "Oh, and tell me who else do you think I'd let touch you like this?" He traced a vein up her arm. "And like this?" His head moved to her midriff and he sucked the tiny indent of her belly button. It tickled and Debra squirmed and giggled. The sound echoed around her head.

"You like that?" His breath teased her skin. "How about this?" He took hold of one hard nipple and rolled it between his fingers.

"Oh yes." She pushed into his hand. His fingers tightened then moved away. The loss of the erotic touch made her whimper.

"Impatient are we? I like that." He bent his head and licked her clit. It was as well his hand was flat on her belly, or Debra would have arched up enough to make a tunnel for a freight train to pass through.

"Now let me see. Oh my, wet for me, ready for me, come for me?" His words reverberated across her pussy, before he licked her sensitive skin once more.

The tingles and stings of pleasure skittered over her skin and into her soul. Her body was on fire as Braam moved across the bed until he lay between her legs. The hairs on his arms tickled her and his scent teased her. She drank it all in and let him fill her senses.

All the while, he played with her nipples as well as keeping up a steady lick and nip to her clit and the opening of her channel. When his tongue inched inside her, Debra bit her lips to hold back her climax. She was oh so wet and wanted to fall over the edge into sensations. However, she wanted Braam with her, in her, so they flew together. Debra dug her heels into the mattress and tried to lift her hips.

Braam wasn't cooperative. Instead the pressure of his lips on her pussy and clit increased and the flick and tease inside her became faster.

He pinched her nipples hard and for a brief second lifted his head.

"This is all for you, love. Come for me now."

The next swipe of his tongue was all she needed. Debra shook with the intensity of emotions that rolled through her like lava. A rainbow of sparks and stars danced behind her eyelids and her skin stung almost to the point of pain as her climax rippled and bounced over her into her and the world stopped. Nothing mattered except his touch and her reaction.

Debra cried. Tears of happiness that Braam was with her. Tears of sorrow that he hadn't come at the same time as her. Soon, she thought as she slowly came back to reality. It'll be his turn to come, my turn to take him there. *Braam moved away and with an inward smirk she rolled after him.*

"My turn now. My turn to make you moan and groan and scream as you come for me." She reached out and felt something soft and cool.

Linen, not flesh. He was wearing too many clothes. Then she had a thought. Not seconds before he'd been naked. His flesh had caressed her as he'd made her come. Something was wrong here.

A loud buzz shot into her brain like a bullet.

The bump as she hit the floor, tangled in a sheet, woke her up with a jolt. Debra blinked. Where was she? No Braam and no familiar room. However, her body was damp, her pussy throbbed and her thighs were coated with her arousal.

Damn and blast. Had it all been a dream? As she woke up properly and remembered where she was and why, Debra switched off the alarm and could have cried.

* * * *

"Mum, when are you going to snap out of whatever snit you're in and looking like you're expecting a Glasgow kiss instead of a sticky grandson one?" Lena MacLeod, Debra's married daughter, wiped the kitchen table down and pointed to the chair beside it. "Sit and spill the beans. Who's got you like this?"

"A what? Who'd want to head thump me? No one's going to give me a Glasgow kiss, love." Debra pulled out a wet wipe and rubbed it over the chubby toddler who sat in his high chair next to her. "Just all jelly baby, ice cream gooey ones, eh, Markus?" Debra kissed the boy who waved his hands.

"G'ma. I love G'ma."

"Of course you do." Debra lifted him out and onto her lap. "So, my sweet, what are we going to do today?"

Lena took her son from his grandmother and sat next to Debra. "We, as in Markus and I, are going to stare, nag and bully you, until you 'fess up. Seriously, Ma, you're scaring me. This is not my mum I'm here with. This is a hollow cardboard cut-out."

"I can't be hollow if I'm a cardboard cut-out," Debra said. "They're one-dimensional."

"Well to be honest, Mum, so are you at the moment. You're doing the bare necessity with no emotion and bugger all involvement as far as I can see. You get back here looking like you've spent the last year in a cave with no light, no food and no interest in anything. You tell me you're fine, but I know for a fact you're not sleeping. You're hardly eating enough to keep a snail alive and all you're doing is going through the motions of everyday life. Are you ill? Are you dying and don't know how to tell me? Hell, Mum, help me out here. I'm worried sick."

The tone, combined with the worried look on Lena's face, impinged on Debra's conscience. Lena had the screwed-up faced, tired-eyed expression of someone who had little sleep for all the wrong reasons. Debra bit the edge of her lip. Tiny, nasty pin pricks of scruples weighed heavily on her mind. Had she genuinely been that bad? Probably. Lena was correct and she needed to snap out of it. Put up or shut up, move on or sort it. If she knew what was the proper thing to do it would be helpful. The trouble was, she didn't, or she wasn't prepared to admit it.

"You know, Mum, you always used to tell me a trouble shared is a trouble halved and goodness knows I've unburdened on you often enough. That's what families do. Moan, cry, listen, offer advice unwanted or not and be there for each other. I'm feeling left out. As if you don't trust me enough to confide in me."

"Oh, Lena." Debra stared at her daughter and burst into tears.

Once she had started, she couldn't stop. Tears were said to be cathartic and these definitely were. Lena pushed a box of tissues across the table toward her and let her cry.

Eventually Debra shuddered and took a deep breath.

"Grief, I needed that."

"I guessed. Look let me put Markus down for his nap and then we'll go into the garden and you can talk. If you want to?" Lena stood up with a sleepy Markus snuggled over her shoulder, his thumb in his mouth. She had a wary expression on her face. It prickled Debra's conscience. She had put it on her daughter's face and it wasn't acceptable.

"I want to." She rolled her shoulders to release the tension and could have cried all over again at the relief that showed on Lena's face. "You put my boy down for a sleep, and sod it, I'm opening a bottle of wine." She was sure she'd need the Dutch courage.

Although, as she walked into the bright sunshine that they had so rarely in this part of Scotland, with a bottle of Sancerre, two glasses and a wine cooler,

Debra reckoned she'd better not drink too much. Over the past week or so, her diet had mainly consisted of eating a few mouthfuls of whatever was put in front of her and once Lena was busy elsewhere, pushing the rest around her plate or offering it to the dog under the table. With that in mind, and also owing to a distinct and unexpected rumble from her tummy, Debra went back indoors to load a tray with crisps and nibbles.

When Lena joined her, she'd set up a low table and added the food, drink and box of tissues to the top.

"Blimey, Mum, have you got a worm or something?" Lena stared at the array. "There's more food on here than you've eaten since you got back."

Debra sniggered and poured two glasses of wine. Maybe she had gone over the top. "Well I have a feeling I'm going to need something to soak up the wine and I'm going to need the wine, a full glass or more."

"Fair enough. So shoot, I'm all ears."

"I met a man," Debra said slowly. She had to do her best to be clear, concise and not make either her or Braam look tacky. Not yet.

"Ah," Lena said, her voice laden with satisfaction. "I told Ronnie that's what it was." Ronnie was her husband, at present serving abroad with Her Majesty's Armed Forces. "Isn't it always? I remember what I was like when Ron and I were trying to get together. So what went wrong? Was he too forward, not forward enough? Too old, too young, not able to get it up? Tell Aunty Lena."

Debra snickered half-heartedly. "Aunty Lena, you're nosy."

Lena sat back in her seat. "Well, there is that as well. With Ronnie away I need to get my kicks and dose of sex chat somehow."

"Kicks?"

"Oh yeah. I read a hot book today. BDSM in Scotland. It was... Well, let's say, I wish Ron had been about. Not that I'm into it, but by God I loved reading it. Talk about a turn-on. But now I've read it so it's up to you to give me my next dose. I've got new batteries in my vibrator all ready and waiting."

"Lena." Debra didn't know whether to laugh or hide her red face. "This is me, your mother who still doesn't think her little girl does anything 'like that'." She mimed quote marks.

Lena giggled. "Then where did Markus and Tristan come from?"

"The stork brought them of course. Put them under a gooseberry bush for you to find."

They both burst out laughing.

"Okay, well, here goes. I met this man in Hong Kong. He's younger than me and..."

"How much younger?" Lena butted in. "Are we talking young enough to be my kid brother sort of young? That would be weird, but hey, if he's who you want, I'll try to look at him and not imagine him in a pram or having his nappy changed when I was still at school."

"It's not that bad. He's maybe eleven or twelve years younger than I am."

"Is that all," Lena let her breath out in a whistle. "That doesn't even make you much of a cougar. Okay, so, you've met a guy. You fancy him?"

"Oh, yes." Debra let herself think about Braam—pre the pregnancy moment Braam—then quashed the way her pussy muscles responded to her thought. "I fancied him." *Although fancy is too mild a word. I need to add…the pants off him, or lust like never before.*

"Does he fancy you?" Lena didn't mention the past tense.

"I thought he did."

"Okay. Now you're worrying me. Did?"

Debra put down her wine glass, ate an olive and schooled her thoughts. "Sheesh, do you know? This is so weird. Me telling you about my love life. Or lust life. Or lack of it."

"Mum, tell me and I'll gross out over it later," Lena said. "So you fancied the pants off each other and I'm guessing you did something about it?"

Oh yeah. "Lots of something."

"Okay, Mum, we don't need all the nitty-gritty. I might be grown up, but you're still my mum and it wouldn't make me go all gooey in a nice way. So what went wrong? What happened?"

Debra blinked away the ready tears that gathered in her eyes. "His pregnant wife happened."

Lena dropped her glass. Luckily it bounced in the grass. Neither of them noticed it.

"I don't believe you. You're too savvy to fall for a cheating scumbag."

Thank goodness for supportive daughters.

Debra shrugged. "I thought so, but I was wrong. Hell, Lena, he was so special," she said morosely. "Or he could have been," she added honestly. "I guess it was all too much too fast for me and on his side all too bloody convenient."

"So what happened? Go on, *now* dish the dirt and clean up the sex." Lena picked up her glass, refilled it and sat back and took a sip of wine. "It's like the agony aunt column in the trashy mags. Or, you know, one of those TV shows. Douchebags of the world get outed. I still think you've got it wrong, though."

"Lena, honey. When a woman throws her arms around a guy and says 'we're pregnant' it sort of shouts 'oh ho parents to be', now, doesn't it? You know waves a *sign* saying 'beware—cheating, lying scumbag'." Debra glared at the food on the table as if it was all its fault. She rummaged through the sticks of celery, chose one, crunched the end of it and waved the rest in the air to make her point. "What I can't understand is how he thought he'd get away with it. For fuck's sake, he works for the hotel and everyone knows him. I was a guest in the hotel and although we didn't go at it like rabbits in the foyer, we didn't exactly skulk behind bushes and use the fire stairs so as not to meet anyone." She blushed. Okay it wasn't the foyer exactly, but Debra went hot and cold when she remembered what they'd gotten up to in the pool.

"Um, why the embarrassed look? Where did you get up to it?" Lena poked Debra on her shoulder. "Come on, dish the dirt. In the corridor? In the lift? In the pool... *Mum*, you devil."

Debra put her hands over her hot cheeks. "Well not quite, but, oh, Lordy, Lena, I almost seduced him."

"Wuss. Only almost? And you call yourself a liberated woman. Why only almost?"

Was she actually discussing explicit things about her sex life to her daughter? It seemed so.

"No condom."

"Fair enough. Okay and then?"

In for a penny. Debra recounted everything. Well almost everything. Some details were best kept to herself.

"And that's it. She announced to the world—well, the hotel—she was pregnant. He broke our date without an explanation and so I cut my losses and went to Singapore. And even the doorman said didn't I think it was great news. What?"

Lena was shaking her head. "You're in love and lost your marbles, Mum. Think about it. The doorman said 'Isn't it good news'? The guy who'd seen you walk in and out. No one sent you dirty looks or whispered behind your back. Braam didn't hide you away like dirty laundry. Everyone thought it was all good. Somewhere you've got the wrong end of the stick. And you didn't bother to find out what the fuck was going on. And yes, I'm swearing at you, you ninny." Lena's voice rose and her words tumbled over each other. "Don't tell me you couldn't have even said something like 'Oh, yes it is. Who is she'? Or something. Hells bells, Mum, what a cock-up you've made. So what are you going to do about it, eh?" She stood up, grabbed a slice of carrot and ate it. A wailing noise came from behind her chair. Lena picked up the intercom.

"Damn it, now Markus is awake and will need changing. And Tristan will be home from school soon. Think about it, Mum. Sort it out somehow, or you'll spend the rest of your life wondering what if. And that's a shite thing to have on your mind. Believe me, until Ronnie and I sorted our life out, I suffered from it. It's nasty."

The wails got louder. "Got to dash. When Markus and I get back, I want your solution." She set off indoors at a run.

Debra sighed and finished off the bowl of cherries, two sticks of celery and half a tub of hummus. She wouldn't mind the solution either. There was no doubt she had to do something, even if it was a basic ask why and say bye. Her problem was how?

She sat in deep thought and rolled questions around her mind without getting any answers. Even if she got in touch with Braam and everything was above board, why should he forgive her? And even more to the point, why trust her? Debra stood up and restlessly wandered around Lena's flower filled garden. The bushes and shrubs were at their late spring best and scents vied with each other to fill the air. A few early bees buzzed from one flower to the next and the noise filled the air in a pleasant think of summer manner.

Debra had no idea how long she was alone with her thoughts until an excited squeal broke into her reverie.

"G'ma. Up." Markus tugged at her arm. "Cuddles."

That was easy. By the time Lena rejoined them, Debra and Markus were rolling over the lawn in gales of laughter as they tickled each other.

"Any thoughts?" Lena went straight to the point.

Debra rolled onto her back and held Markus high in the air over her head. He giggled and kicked as they made vroom vroom aircraft noises.

"Oh, I'm going to have to see him somehow. Even if it's purely to say sorry I ran. And if it's true, to restrain myself from making sure he goes forth and multiplies no more."

"Right. Well, good to both of those. And this should help." Lena handed her a slip of paper. "I couldn't run to business class, but they said you can upgrade if you want. It's a single ticket on tomorrow evening's flight to Hong Kong."

She did. In her state of nervous anxiety, Debra accepted it wasn't fair to inflict a wriggling, wide awake, anxiety ridden woman next to some poor unsuspecting passenger.

* * * *

"Well I think you're a thick idiot," Jack said as he and Braam sat in a favorite bar in Sai Kung and waited for Kris to come back from a bargain-hunting foray. "What were you thinking with? Your gonads? Hell, Braam, Kris had announced she was pregnant, I'd added to it and you just told your lady you had to cry off. Why?"

Braam shrugged, once again feeling the younger brother who never did anything right.

"Because I wanted to ask you first. Then introduce her to you both as someone important."

"And instead I bet you a weekend in Paris she heard me shouting *we* were pregnant to you." Kris dropped several bulging carrier bags and a couple of boxes onto the table. She flopped into the chair and took a defiant slurp from her husband's beer glass. "I bet she thought you were all kinds of shite and cut and ran. Anyone would. It sounded more than dodgy. I made you look like every sort of two-timing creep. You need to go to her."

"No I don't. Either she trusts me or she doesn't." Braam knew his voice was harsh, but didn't they realize how her lack of trust had almost emasculated him? He'd wanted to scream and shout and race after her. When he saw a new guest being ushered into her room, he had been shattered. Up until then, Braam had held on to the hope that she *had* gone to visit friends and was returning to the hotel. As he had no intention of adding to the hotel gossip mill, he'd checked the register once the day staff had left and seen the damning words *'paid in full'* across her invoice. Even now, his gut churned and it made him feel sick. "I'm not going anywhere to get my head kicked in."

"Bloody hell, men. Braam Van Meister, are you a man or a mouse?" Kris asked him. She looked like a ferocious kitten. All flashing eyes and spitting.

"Mouse," Braam and Jack said together. Kris rolled her eyes.

"That's for sure. Anyway it's called a Glasgow kiss over there. You know, getting your head kicked in. Well, nutted, but that's what they call it. And I wouldn't blame her, because seriously you made a right pig's ear of it." She sat back in her seat. "And I'd like a Jasmine tea please."

"Does she ever get fed up of giving advice?" Braam asked Jack with a wry grin.

Jack shook his head. "Nah and in this case I reckon she's spot on. Mind you I'd wear a box and maybe body armor."

Braam loved his brother and sister-in-law, but at that moment, he could see them far enough, as the saying went. He had enough to worry over without their suggestions. He'd traced the missing manager, but sadly not the money. The guy was stubbornly silent over what he'd done with it. There was going to be a lot of hard work by a lot of people over the following months to get that mess sorted out. Braam himself had been working sixteen-hour days and they weren't all down to keeping himself busy so he couldn't mope. Today was a rare break and he'd taken it solely because Kris had said she was worried and worry was bad for pregnant women and the babies they carried. Even though Braam knew it was out and out blackmail, he had accepted why she'd said it and had accompanied her and Jack out to the fishing village. It had also given him a chance to check up on his house. He was beginning to forget what it looked like.

"I'm busy. I have a job to do." And don't say any more, his tone warned.

Kris opened her mouth and Braam saw Jack shake his head.

"All I was going to ask is when and where we're eating," she said in an injured tone. "I'll have my tea with food. I'm hungry."

Jack guffawed. "When are you ever not? What do you reckon, Braam? Do we feed her? It'll shut her up for a bit at least."

"Definitely feed her then. Come on, let's go to Chicona's and Kris can make you groan when she tells you everything she's bought and ordered."

"Oh yes, let's."

Braam had to smile as he paid the bill and followed them out of the bar. Their love was easy to see and he envied them. It was what he'd hoped he and Debra would have. However… *Don't go there.*

He shoved his wallet back into his pocket and increased his pace to catch up with the other couple.

"So, any names yet?"

Jack groaned. "Don't even mention names. I reckon it will be ones neither of us are genuinely enamored of, but we at least agree they're not bad."

"Jacob Van Meister, I am not having a child called Augustus or Archibald. Make a note so you remember. I want nice easy to write and not get wrong names, like Lucy, or Lily, or Jack and Braam. Only Bram with one 'a'. Don't you agree, Braam?" Kris appealed to her brother-in-law.

Braam held his hands up. She hung two carrier bags over them and giggled.

"Don't involve me," Braam said. "I've enough problems of my own without getting involved in your squabbles. I'd go for A, B, C, D and so on." He ducked Kris' mock punch. "Come on, we're here. Let's eat."

Later he had no idea what he'd eaten. All he knew was that by the time he got back to the hotel, he was antsy and he didn't know why. He should put in a couple more hours in the office but acknowledged that in the mood he was in, he'd be next to useless. Braam checked his emails, both work wise and personal, and saw there was nothing that was urgent. In his mind, he knew that nothing urgent translated into nothing from Debra.

He poured a gluten free beer and after one sip tipped it down the sink. He didn't want alcohol, he wanted Debra. He admitted to himself that he'd done everything the wrong way and he'd love the chance to put it right. Kris' advice echoed around his head. *'Go to her'*. He shook his head and washed the glass up. Stubborn or stupid, it hurt that she hadn't waited to hear his explanation.

Sod it, I'll go for a swim. He looked at the clock. *Yeah it's closed, but hey, what's the point of having a pass key if I don't use it?* He'd been swimming at night more and more often. Length after length to chase the demons and the hard-on away. If nothing else, he would wear himself out and not spend all night reaching for a hot female body that was in his imagination only. He was sick of cold showers.

With his mind made up, Braam stripped and changed into his trunks. One of the perks of having his accommodation on that floor was its proximity to the roof garden and pool.

He tucked his key card and phone into a zippered bag and left the room to walk outside.

The air was warm and humid and the sky clear. He could imagine the length of the queues to get the tram up to the peak to enjoy the view of the city. Apart from that, the waterside would be packed with people waiting to see the laser show that happened every evening. Lovers and couples and families all were enjoying the beautiful weather.

Sod that. A pity fest is not on. He walked across the sitting area toward the gate to the pool.

It was ajar and he could hear splashing.

Déjà vu?

Braam pushed open the gate and walked toward the pool.

Definitely déjà vu.

Whoever it was swimming couldn't sing for toffee. The off key rendition of 'Gonna Wash That Man Right Out Of My Hair' should have made him smile. Instead it lodged a great big lump of worry inside him. Once again the singer stopped mid verse and there was a loud splash then silence. A few bubbles popped up from the depths, but the singer-swimmer was nowhere to be seen.

He waited anxiously as the seconds passed. Nothing, all he could fix his eyes on were those damned bubbles. *Shit, had she drowned singing that stupid song?* Not again.

"Well, look what the cat dragged in." She surfaced, spoke, then did a perfect roll under the water and he caught a glimpse of bright red underwear—yet again there was no way on earth the scraps of lace were a bikini—before she popped up again and pushed her dark hair out of her eyes. "Gonna try to wash your sins away? It doesn't work."

"Tell me about it. Nor do cold showers when I wake up hard and horny and reaching for you."

"Yep, so... What we going to do about it?" She rolled onto her back and swam in lazy circles. Her bare breasts peeped in and out of the water as if they were playing Hide and Seek. "Do I make sure you never have any more kids?"

"Be difficult to have any more when I haven't got any already. I'm going to be an uncle, not a father." He couldn't help but get a grain of satisfaction at the way her eyes widened and she gasped. "That scene I assume you saw was my sister-in-law telling the world she and my brother are to be parents. She asked me to keep it quiet. I wanted to ask them if I could tell you and would have explained later. If you'd been around. Look, this is not the place to let me grovel and I accept I need to." Could she understand the pleading in his tone? He hoped so.

Debra stared up at him. The water glistened on her skin and the moonlight sent shards of light dancing around her. She looked like a water nymph.

"So why don't you join me? Or is jogging the only exercise you do?" She tilted her head to one side and like before, swam in lazy circles around the island in the center of the pool.

Does she know there's innuendo in that statement?

"Come on, live dangerously. We can talk later. I've got my own explaining to do. But first? You know you shouldn't swim alone at night." She laughed. "So we'll be helping each other in actual fact."

Braam dove in and swam toward her. "So... Hello, Ms. Intruder. We meet again."

"It seems we do. What happens next?"

"This." He bent his head and kissed her.

Chapter Twelve

Oh, Lord, it's a romance novel moment. It was funny how your mind came up with stupid thoughts at important times in your life.

As Braam moved closer to her and blocked out the night sky, Debra closed her eyes and let herself become lost in her own world of heat and arousal. Even her scalp tingled. The moment his lips touched hers, Debra's pussy contracted. If she hadn't been wet from the water, she'd be wet from her arousal. Her nipples ached and her clit throbbed. Every nerve was standing on end as they begged for attention.

The water swirled around them and held them captive. She hooked her legs around Braam's waist and let him carry her wherever he wanted. Deep inside her, a tiny voice of reason said she should slow things down and they aught to talk. In the mood she was in—hot and aroused—she quashed it. Reason later, touch, feel and taste now.

Almost as if it was an effort, Braam ended the kiss and tilted his head back enough for Debra to see him clearly.

"Shit, love. I promised myself if I saw you again, I'd explain properly and grovel. Then jump you." He swallowed heavily and his breathing was choppy. "I..." He shook his head and droplets of water sparkled and shone like a white and silver rainbow above them.

Debra laughed. Her heart was now lighter and definitely beat faster.

"You groveled rather well, I think." She tightened her legs and he edged closer. "In fact, perhaps you'd like to do a bit more?"

She waited whilst he studied her face, then oh so slowly ran his finger down her cheek and across her lips. "Oh yes, but perhaps not in here?"

A very theatrical cough made them both jump.

"Definitely not in here. Get a room both of you. This is a tad too public for what I reckon you're both thinking. Of course, it has nothing to do with what I'm hoping to get up to with Jack."

The pregnant lady Debra had last seen clinging to Braam like a limpet stood on the edge of the pool wearing a bikini that emphasized the gentle swell of her stomach. Next to her was the man she'd been clinging to at Sai Kung. Debra flattened the immediate surge of jealously that flared up when she saw how radiant the woman was and how both men looked at her with different degrees of affection. Oh, she believed Braam, there was no doubt about it, but if only he'd look at her like the other guy did at the lady.

"Debra, this is Kris and Jack," Braam said and laughed as he moved behind her and covered her bare breasts with his arms. His hard cock rubbed the cleft of her ass and she leaned back to appreciate the feeling even more. He tightened his hold on her and held her close. "Proud parents to be and mega meddlers."

"Hey, not me," the man—Jack—said with a tone of mock horror in his voice. "It's all Kris and her cloak and dagger stuff that's caused all the problems."

"No it's not," Debra said firmly. She had never been one to let other people be responsible for her own mistakes. "It was me and my lack of trust. I should have asked straight away who the blonde bombshell in blue plastered all over Braam was and not jumped to conclusions. Then when he canceled our date asked why. Not meekly stood back, simmered, stewed and ran. Mind you, I did run to somewhere nice."

Kris sat down on the side of the pool and let her legs dangle in the water. She moved them back and forth and created waves that slapped against the walls.

"Hi, Debra. Blonde bombshell in blue, eh? I must remember that. Welcome to the Van Meister Madhouse. Mama Van M and I need you to even up the numbers." She waved her hand in greeting. "This is Jacob, the other but not always wiser Van Meister brother. Proud daddy to be and about to make me a happy mummy to be. I need chocolate."

Jack hooted. "I thought you said you needed sun lounger by the pool sex?"

"Jack," Kris went the color of Debra's knickers. "Shut up."

Debra decided it was time to say something. "Er, well, hello, I'm Debra and I've been enjoying Braam's groveling." She ignored Kris' snort and muttered, "Oh, another new word for it."

"Seriously, it's all down to me and my insecurity. My, how on earth can a ho—well, a man like Braam, fancy an older woman like me," she said hurriedly.

"And on that note, we're off to talk somewhere *private*. Talk, Kris." He emphasized the word. "So buzz off for a minute and let us get out and disappear. Then the pool is all yours. Remember to lock up behind yourselves and if you get caught, don't get me to bail you out, okay?"

"Well, that's family solidarity." Kris grinned as she said it.

"You bet. Now clear off for five minutes."

"Come on, sweetie, let's walk around the garden and spare their blushes." Jack took her arm and led her out of the pool area.

"Blushes?" Debra asked.

"Yeah, my hard-on is about ripping my trunks and your nipples are digging into my arms. As much as I'd love to rip off whatever you've got on and see if making love in the water is all it's reported as it's cracked up to be, I want you all to myself with no interruptions. I reckon your room?"

Debra ducked under the water and out of his arms and swam to the edge. She heaved herself up out of the pool and stood up to let the water drip off her onto the tiles. Braam followed her and ran his hand over her breast to flick a bead of liquid from her still hard nipple.

"As much as I want to take this lusciousness in my mouth, I'm going to restrain myself. For now. Do you have a robe?"

Debra pointed. "Over there. And you might want to reconsider the my room bit. It's the same as last time and I'm sure that's the floor your brother and his wife are on?"

"God, yes, come on, let's plot." He picked up Debra's robe and held it out for her to slip into. Then took her hand and dragged her over to the lift.

"Diversionary tactics are about to happen. Watch." He called the lift, nipped inside then pressed the ground floor button before he got out again. The doors closed and the lift descended.

"Right into the corridor to my room and don't say a word." Braam towed her toward the door they needed and within seconds had opened it, pushed her in front of him and followed her inside. He shut the door and beckoned to her to stand close to him.

"I bet you we'll hear Kris complaining we've gone down to the foyer so she doesn't know where we are." He spoke very quietly in her ear. "And no one can get into this corridor without a special code or buzzing my suite. We won't answer. That'll drive her crazy."

"You, Mr. Van M, are a devious man." Debra turned her head to whisper back to him. "I love it."

He gently nipped her earlobe with his teeth. "Yeah? Good, shh, I can hear something."

They stood facing each other, one ear to the door, like a pair of kids playing couples hide and seek, or Seven Seconds in Heaven.

"The bugger, look the lifts are at ground. Both of them. I bet he did that on purpose so there would be no chance of me working out where they are. Sod it." Kris' light, clear voice came clearly through the door. "I mean surely they know I'm going to be too busy seducing you to annoy them?"

Jack's voice came as a rumble that Debra couldn't decipher.

"Oh, well, then, in that case…" Kris laughed, then there was silence.

"In that case," Braam said as they walked away from the door toward his room. "We can talk."

Debra hoped they were going to do a lot more than that, but she accepted that talk had to come first.

"Wine? Or tea?" Braam ushered her into his suite and closed and locked the door. "I think maybe wine?"

Oh, yes. "Please, because it's now my turn to grovel. I was an idiot." Debra took the glass of wine Braam handed her. "Thanks. But you know a woman in..." she hesitated. *Oh what the hell, I've almost bared my body in the pool, I might as well go for broke and bare my soul.* "A woman in love doesn't always think in a rational way. I'd been so looking forward to seeing you and telling you about my day. Then I had great plans on how I could seduce you and well... Well."

She shrugged and sighed. "I saw Kris throw herself at you and say you were going to be parents. So I ran. After all I'm older, widowed, but *not* needy. I've got kids and grandchildren and no way was I going to be the other woman. When you blew me off with no explanation, I came to the conclusion I was right. So I left. Then I saw you in Central with Kris and no one else, so in my mind that reinforced everything that I'd seen and heard. It wasn't until I eventually got back to Scotland that I wondered if I had the wrong end of the stick. And Lena took me apart and gave me what for. She said I was a wuss and a coward and her mum had taught her better than that. Then told me in no uncertain terms I should practice what I preach and presented me with a one-way ticket and a hotel confirmation in her name. I got in this afternoon. Then I sort of made sure the door was unlocked to the pool and crossed my fingers."

"What would you have done if I didn't go for a swim?" Braam asked her with a curious note in his voice.

Debra shrugged. "Well, my plan B was to shout for help over the intercom... Say I'd got stuck or something and wait for someone, hopefully you, to rescue me. If that didn't work, plan C was to find you and do this. I'm so glad I didn't find you in the foyer." Very slowly she untied her gown and let it drop to the floor. "But I cheated. Simon, the night manager, said you were up swimming most nights." She hoped her trembles weren't noticeable—seducing a man hadn't been high up in her repertoire—as she ran her hands across her breasts and down her sides and hooked her thumbs in the sides of her still damp from the pool knickers. The way his nostrils flared and the pulse in his neck showed gave her optimism.

If only she knew what to do next.

"Don't look so worried," Braam said hoarsely. "Do you know what a turn-on this is?" He glanced down at the tent in his shorts and up at her face once more.

"I don't know how," Debra owned up. "But if you directed me?"

"Oh, I can do that, love. Ditch the knicks."

"Like this?" She wriggled and squirmed until her undies were around her ankles and kicked them away. Would he notice how she'd trimmed her pussy hair? Would he care?

"What next?"

"Ah... Er, damn, Deb, that is so beautiful I could stand here and stare at you for hours." His eyes darkened and the arousal he experienced was obvious, even to someone with limited experience, like Debra. He winked and swallowed heavily. His Adam's apple moved the skin of his throat and he licked his lips.

It was one of the most heartening, hot and arousing acts Debra had ever watched. She, Debra Scotburn, made him feel like that. If she hadn't felt her boobs would almost hit her in the face she would have jumped up and fisted the air and shouted Yee-har. Instead she grinned and gave a silly mock curtsey. "I aim to please."

"Oh, you more than please. My cock might not wait long to be pleased as well. So, next take my shorts off for me. Careful, there's something in the way. We might, well I hope we might, need it later."

So did Debra.

She bit her lip as she concentrated and maneuvered the wet fabric down Braam's ass and over his cock. It sprang up like a jack-in-a-box and waved from side to side. Debra giggled.

"He does seem happy to see me." She tugged on the shorts and tried not to wince as Braam grimaced when her hands scraped his thighs. "Sorry, does it hurt?"

He shook his head. "Apart from in a God I want you now, my pre-cum is shouting I want out of you, let me in her sort of way. That is a pain well worth having, especially as the end result will be pleasure."

She hoped so.

It was strange to walk naked like she was, Debra mused, and not worry about a wobbly tummy or swaying breasts. Well not to worry too much. It was also liberating.

No more secrets.

She took the opportunity to use the facilities and clean her teeth before she went back to Braam.

When she got back, the lounge was empty, but the door to the bedroom was half open.

"In here," Braam's voice reached her from inside the bedroom. "I thought I'd get the bed all comfy for us."

"Good thinking, Batman." Debra walked out of the lounge and gasped. He'd lit candles, lots of candles that flickered and danced in the air. On a table next to the bed were two flutes and a bottle of champagne cooling in a bucket of ice and a bowl of fruit.

Braam picked a strawberry up out of the bowl, dipped it into one of the glasses and held it out to her. "I've always wanted to do this," he said. "Ever since I saw *Pretty Woman*, but I've never had my own pretty woman to do it with. I wasn't sure if strawberries were your thing, so I hedged my bets. You can have raspberry, melon, apple and paw-paw instead if you'd prefer."

She burst out laughing. "Strawberries are perfect." Debra took the few steps needed to reach the bed and leaned over him so he could put the fruit in her mouth. "Oh yum." The soft sweet fruit with a hint of sparkling champagne on its skin was perfect. The combination of sharp and sweet and the two different but complementary aromas were perfect. It was difficult to know whether to inhale or swallow.

"Now your turn." Debra selected a plump strawberry and dipped it slowly into a glass of fizzy bubbles. She watched as the liquid covered it and dripped slowly back into the flute. She held it to Braam's mouth and rubbed the soft ripe fruit over his lips before holding it steady.

"Taste that."

He opened his mouth and let her thread the fruit inside.

"I do think you'd be happier lying down now," he said gravely and patted the bed next to him.

"You do? Why?" Intrigued, Debra scrambled up next to him and stretched out with her head on a pillow.

"So I can do this. Don't wriggle." He picked up one of the glasses and slowly tilted it over her stomach.

She didn't wriggle. Debra gasped and moaned in delight as drop by drop, the champagne hit her heated skin. So slowly that it could have been a film run at half speed, Braam chose his spot and let the liquid fall.

One drop on each nipple and several in her belly button and a steady stream over her pussy lips.

He put the glass down. "Now it's time I had a drink. All this groveling is thirsty work."

"Oh, yes, I'm sure it is. I think I need a drink as well. Something salty and tasty?"

Braam laughed. "Oh you'll get some later, never fear, but first." He dipped his head and licked one of her nipples. His rough tongue stroked over her sensitive skin. The sensation, like an electric shock, made her jump and her pussy muscles tighten as she held back the trembles that began to fill her. Her juices gathered and mingled with the liquid Braam had coated her with and she moaned in delight.

Coherent thought was beyond her, as she watched Braam nip and suck each of her nipples in turn. Debra wriggled. Those tiny touches sent the invisible chord of arousal that was connected to her clit into overdrive. He chuckled, put his head onto her tummy and licked the champagne in her navel.

"Careful, we don't want to lose any now, do we?"

I don't mind. Not if it means you do it all again.

He took his time and traced a path with his tongue from her naval to her clit. With one hand he tweaked each nipple in turn and with the other played with her pussy. Debra let her eyes close and became absorbed in his touch.

Nothing existed except his scent, his touch and those ever increasing spirals of need that streaked through her. When he sucked her clit and put two fingers into her channel, she screamed with pleasure. It was impossible to control the red-hot fire that filled her and pushed her over the edge into a fierce and furious climax.

"Now, fill me now." She sobbed the words and tugged at Braam's hair as he continued to lick and nip her clit and her pussy. "Please, Braam, now."

He moved. Even before Debra had the chance to mourn the loss of his touch, she felt the tip of his cock pushing at the entrance to her pussy.

"Legs. My shoulders. Please." He spoke in a staccato burst. Debra lifted her legs and her bum slid over the coverlet. Then Braam pushed forward and her body opened eagerly to welcome him.

"Oh, yeah…" It was all she could manage to say as he moved his cock inside her. The friction, the tightness and the sheer joy of knowing they were together like that once more increased her arousal. Debra matched Braam thrust for thrust. She reveled in the grunts and harsh breathing she heard.

When she reached up and took one of his nipples between her thumb and forefinger, he shuddered and beads of sweat dotted his skin. Debra laughed softly as a sensation of power swept over her. She made this man feel like that. Her body and her touch affected him.

When she gave the other nipple the same attention, Braam groaned.

"Sweet Lord, woman. Do you *know* what that does to me? I'm going to have to come, now."

Those were the words she wanted to hear. As he surged into her and filled her as far as possible, Debra let her own climax build to the point of no return.

Hot, greedy need swelled inside her and Debra let it. Braam's eyes were half closed and his face a study of concentration and absorption. As she closed her own eyes to experience every last ounce of tension and arousal without anything to disturb it, Braam shuddered and shouted his release.

It tipped Debra over the edge and she joined him in the vortex. Her mind went blank, she saw stars and the ringing in her ears got louder and louder. Then everything went black.

She came back to consciousness to the sound of Braam swearing.

Her eyelids were heavy, and if someone had told her they were glued together, she could easily have accepted it. With more effort than she thought possible, Debra opened them and looked into Braam's worried, pale face as he loomed over her. She realized with a jolt they were no longer joined and the cool sheet was beneath her back and her head rested on the pillow. He'd tucked the sheet over her so her head and shoulders were bare to the cool air.

"Thank God. Hell, woman, you scared the life out of me. Are you all right?" His voice was full of anxiety. "I didn't know whether to throw water on you or call an ambulance. You came like a lion, muttered something I didn't get and half closed your eyes. Then you were out for the count. Talk about withdrawal symptoms. I hope to hell I didn't hurt you."

Debra blinked and considered her body and how it and she felt. Sated.

"Oh, no. And I can honestly say that in all of my forty-four years I have never quite had such an extreme little death before." She smiled and ran her finger over his cheek in the way he so often did to her. "Amazing and oh so special. Thank you."

Some of the worry left his face and his pallor decreased. "You're welcome, I think. I swear, though,

I aged twenty years. I've never felt so helpless in my life. Are you really okay?"

"Really," Debra said. "Except I'm all sticky and I... What? *What?*" Braam had lost what little color he'd regained. "Tell me, Braam, *what?* Hell don't faint on me."

"Sticky. I came inside you."

"Well good, that was the whole point of the exercise, wasn't it? To come in me and... Oh, fuck."

"Oh, yes. Oh, fuck. Well, we did, didn't we?" Braam's voice was full of self annoyance. "And without a condom."

Debra had worked that out for herself. She frantically added dates and days up in her mind. "Well," she said with a note of caution evident. "I think I'm okay. So no need to worry about being a daddy." She wished now she hadn't thrown her pills into the Singapore River in a fit of pique.

Braam pinched her bum and she squealed. "What was that in aid of?"

"I'm not worried about being a daddy." His voice rose. "In fact, one day I'd love to be a daddy as long as you're the mummy and you want it too. And before you prattle on about the age difference, I know it might not happen and that's fine as well. But I want to be a married dad. Married to you and that would make me a dad anyway, would— Deb? Shit, woman, say something, don't look at me like I'm an alien. Say something." He put his hand on her arm.

Debra shook his hand off and sat up to see him better. The sheet slipped off her and she tugged at it impatiently before she pressed her ears. Such a silly thing to do, but was she hearing correctly? He wanted to marry her, children or not?

"You're mad. You hardly know me, I'm twelve years older and my kids are almost the same age as you. I honestly don't know if I want to go through sleepless nights and potty training all over again, let alone hormonal teens in a continuous snit." She slid out of bed. "Why on earth would you want to be with me, when you can have anyone? Hell, Braam, do you even know what you're saying?" She hated the way she sniped at him, but seriously?

"It's twelve years, not twenty. I don't think you started your family at that age. Watch my lips. I love you. Why? Goodness knows, I just do." He rolled his eyes and tugged her hair, hard enough to make her wince.

"Ouch."

"I wanted to make sure you're concentrating."

Debra was. Something told her the next few minutes may well be the most important in her life.

"Actually," Braam said. "I do know why. You're funny, serious, quirky, loyal, hot, hot and yeah hot."

"And you know all that, how?" Her heart beat faster and her skin prickled as she waited to hear what he replied.

"What the 'oh, how I love you let me count the ways sort of thing'?" Braam kissed her nose.

It tickled and she wrinkled it. "Yep, that." Not for anything dare she admit she was in pretty much the same state over him.

"Well, let's see. For a start off even when you thought the worst, you put other people first. You heard Kris say she was pregnant and didn't do anything to upset her."

"Of course not," Debra said indignantly. "Nothing was her fault. I couldn't confront you and involve her."

"Exactly. So, kind, compassionate and caring."

Debra wriggled and made herself more comfortable. She was sitting on a damp part of the sheet and it was sticky. "Yuk, how come I'm on the wet bit? Never mind, go on. I have no idea who you're describing, but I like it. Mind you, I'll get a big head at this rate."

"Never. Now where was I? You've broken my thread."

"Um, you were saying how nice I was and about to offer to sit on the sticky bit of sheet?"

"Nope. I'm going to turn on the shower. And I guess take the sheet to the laundry. Luckily I opted not to have housekeeping, or I can imagine the stories going about." He straightened up and smiled. "Think about it, love. I'll wait until you're ready, but take it as your first proposal from me. I'd like it to be the one you say yes to, but if not, expect another. And another, until you give in. It'll be a bit like a dripping tap."

"I'd not say yes because I reckoned it was the best way to shut you up." How could he think that? "If and I repeat *if* I say yes, it's because I think it's right for both of us."

Braam nodded. "Good. Are you going to say yes?"

Debra scrambled of the bed and stood next to him. There was no way she was going to make one of the biggest decisions of her life sitting on a damp bed sheet, with sticky thighs, needing the loo and probably smelling of sex to boot.

"Give me two minutes." She walked past him and went into the bathroom to have a quick wash and brush her teeth. Debra looked in the mirror. As she'd suspected, her hair was all over the place and in her mind, she looked like a cat who had gotten the cream. Happy, satisfied and sated. She finger combed her hair and grabbed two of the toweling robes that hung on the back of the door. There was no way she could tell her kids or grandchildren that she had answered a marriage proposal whilst she and the man in question were both naked. With a giggle—she could imagine Lena high fiving her and Kevan rolling his eyes—she put one on and belted it. Then she carried the other one over her arm, left the bathroom and went into the lounge.

Braam stood next to the fridge with two flutes of champagne in his hands.

"I thought we might need this. Either to celebrate or for me to drown my sorrows. Have you made up your mind?"

Debra waved the robe. "You must be cold."

He put the flutes down and laughed. "Not at all. My cock is knackered, not freezing. Do you want me to turn the air con off?"

Duh, men can be so thick at times.

"No, I want you to put this on and ask me again."

"Eh?" He sounded confused. "About the air con?"

Debra rolled her eyes and punched his shoulder. "Oh, yeah. No, you nit, the down on one knee and propose thing. But not naked."

"I think I'm gonna add weird to my list of things I love about you." Braam shrugged into the robe and left it loose. The look in his eye told Debra he'd done it on purpose.

Every time he moved, his cock showed through the gap and each view told Debra it wasn't half as knackered as the time before.

"Okay, hold on." Braam knelt on one knee and took hold of Debra's hand.

"So, love. Will you marry me?"

She counted to ten, very slowly and tilted her head to one side.

"Hmm, let me see. You're sure you want a much older woman, with kids, who's weird, as your wife?"

"Minx." He tugged her hand. "Put me out of my misery. This floor is hard."

"Yes."

"Yes?"

She nodded. "Oh, yes."

He pulled her until she unbalanced and they tumbled onto the carpet together in a tangle of limbs and toweling robes. Braam rolled over until Debra was stretched on top of him. His cock rubbed her tummy and she wriggled.

"Hmm, someone's not knackered anymore."

"Someone—" Braam kissed her. "Is oh so happy and…"

The room phone and his mobile rang simultaneously, and he groaned. "What's the betting that's Kris and Jack? Shall we tell them our good news? Or make them wait and carry on?"

"Oh, definitely carry on."

He grinned. "Oh, good. Now where were we? Ah yes. My cock is happy and…"

About the Author

A multi-published author of erotic romance, Raven lives in Scotland, along with her husband and their two cats—their children having flown the nest—surrounded by beautiful scenery, which inspires a lot of the settings in her books.

She is used to sharing her life with the occasional deer, red squirrel, and lost tourist, to say nothing of the scourge of Scotland—the midge. As once she is writing she is oblivious to everything else, her lovely long-suffering husband is learning to love the dust bunnies, work the Aga, and be on stand-by with a glass of wine.

Raven McAllan loves to hear from readers. You can find her contact information, website details and author profile page at http://www.totallybound.com.

Totally Bound Publishing